Other series by

LUTHER

This dangerously handsome, effortlessly stylish half-demon is Chicago's foremost paranormal investigator. With magical aptitude and specialized weapons, Luther Cross will handle your supernatural problems... for the right price.

THE MYTH HUNTER

All the legends of the world have some element of truth to them. And to track down those legends, there are the myth hunters. Some, like Elisa Hill, are explorers, trying to learn more about the world. And some are soldiers of fortune, whose only goal is profit and exploitation, no matter the risk.

INFERNUM

A shadowy, globe-spanning network of operatives run by the mysterious power broker known as Dante. They hold allegiance to no one, existing as rogues on the fringes of society. No matter the job, Infernum has an operative to execute it—provided you have the means to pay for it!

VANGUARD

The world has changed. A mysterious event altered the genetic structure of humanity, granting a small percentage of the population superhuman powers. A small team of these specials has been formed to deal with potential threats. Paragon—telekinetic powerhouse; Zenith—hyper-intelligent automaton; Shift—shape-changing teenager; Wraith—teleporting shadow warrior; Sharkskin—human/shark hybrid. Led by the armored Gunsmith, they are Vanguard!

Visit PercivalConstantine.com for an up-to-date list of titles!

Published by Pulp Corner Press

http://www.percivalconstantine.com

A MORNINGSTAR NOVEL

LUCIFER DAMNED

BY PERCIVAL CONSTANTINE

CHAPTER 1

Andrew Greene had been having a good night. He came out to the Red Lion in Lincoln Square hoping for some good drinks, decent food, and with any luck, a chance for some female companionship. His boss had been on a tear on everyone in the office for the past week to finish their projects before the end of the quarter. Stockholders were getting impatient, which meant so were the higher-ups. And that led to crunch time for everyone else.

But it was Friday and Andrew could at least put that out of his mind for the weekend. And he'd managed to do just that. Standing at the crowded bar and sipping a Guinness, he somehow found himself capable of beginning a conversation with Haley. She said she was a graduate student at the University of Chicago. Andrew had barely finished his undergraduate degree at Southern Illinois University, so right from the start it was obvious that Haley had the edge as far as intelligence was concerned.

Fortunately, Andrew had felt renewed confidence thanks to a little bit of work he'd had done on himself. In the six months since then, he hadn't had much luck, but tonight he was feeling good. Haley was in her early twenties with chin-length brown hair and green eyes. She had a great body and Andrew was starting to feel confident as she laughed at his jokes.

"Hey…" she said, reaching her hand for her drink. But instead of taking hold of her glass, she brushed her fingers against his hand, which held his own beer. Andrew felt a charge and looked up at her. There was something about those eyes that he kept finding himself being swept up in. Her smile was different than before, a little more sultry. And then she said those words Andrew had been hoping to hear ever since he spotted her: "You wanna get out of here?"

"Wh-what did you have in mind?" asked Andrew.

Haley blushed and smiled as she looked down at the counter and swept a few strands of hair behind her ear. "Well…" She looked just slightly embarrassed when she leaned in closer and said in a softer voice, "my roommate's out of town this weekend."

A tingle of feeling in Andrew's lower regions responded to Haley's invitation. When she made eye contact with him again and asked, "What do you say?"

Andrew's response was to finish what was left of his Guinness and set the glass down on the counter. "Where do you live?" he asked.

Haley chuckled at his exuberance and finished her own beer. They left the counter and pushed through the crowded bar to reach the exit. Outside, the air was crisp. Despite it technically being spring, it sometimes took the Chicago weather a few weeks to catch up with the season. Haley shivered and Andrew jumped on the opportunity by wrapping his arm around her shoulders.

"Thanks," she said with a smile as she leaned her head

against his chest. "I'm not far, just a little past Western."

Andrew smiled and the pair walked a few blocks down to the corner of Lawerence and Western. As they waited for the light to change, Andrew glanced around, suddenly feeling the odd sense that they weren't alone. There were other people around, sure, but it was almost like they were being watched. Andrew looked at the people who waited at the light and further back down the street towards the bar. Nothing seemed out of the ordinary.

The light changed and Haley pulled him to cross. He gave one more quick survey and then acquiesced. Once across the street, they went another block, but Andrew's sense that they weren't alone persisted. He tried to dismiss it as simple nerves and instead allowed Haley to take him down one of the side streets. She then pulled him into an alley.

"C'mon, my building's just down here. This is a short-cut, we can go in through the back."

"Yeah, sure…" said Andrew, still feeling the growing sense of dread. Better to get off the street quickly in case they were being followed. Last thing he needed was to get mugged right in front of Haley. He wasn't much of a fighter and she'd likely feel humiliated if she saw him cower before some gang banger.

Haley stopped right by the back gate of a small tene-ment. She grabbed Andrew by his jacket and slammed him against the bars. He was shocked at first, but then relaxed once she kissed him. Andrew's hands found her back and he fell into the kiss. Haley's body crushed against him and Andrew felt his body warming to her touch.

"We should go inside…" he said.

Haley nodded. "Yeah, inside." She turned towards the

gate and reached inside her purse, rummaging around for the keys. When she pulled them out and searched for the right one, but they slipped from her hands. "Damn, sorry. Butterfingers," she said and knelt down to pick them up.

Andrew was feeling impatient. Not only because he was excited for what was about to happen, but also because he still felt nervous for what might be out there. And as he looked around, he noticed a guy turn down the alley and start walking towards them. The man was tall and wore a knit cap pulled down to his brow, his chin tucked into his chest to maintain warmth. Not only was he tall, but his shoulders were broad. And there was something about him that made Andrew feel paranoid.

"So…you got that door open yet?" Andrew asked.

"Sorry, give me a sec," said Haley. "This lock's a little tricky, I keep telling the super to fix it, but he just says he'll get to it soon."

The man was coming closer to them. And now he looked up, making eye contact with Andrew. It could have been a trick of the light, but something seemed strange with his eyes. There was almost a kind of flash Andrew could have sworn he saw, as if the eyes had glowed for just a moment.

The man broke contact and continued on. Andrew let out the breath he'd been clutching and turned back to Haley. It was just paranoia, nothing more. He had to get himself together, didn't want Haley to think he was some pussy who'd flinch at the first sign of a stranger.

"Hey."

Andrew's body stiffened when he heard the sound. He turned around and saw that same man walking towards him. The guy came closer, almost towering over him. Andrew swallowed hard and reached for the pocket that held his wallet, willing to just hand it over quickly.

The guy's hands were in his pockets. Slowly, he pulled one of them out. Andrew started to shrink down, fearing that it might be a knife or maybe even a gun. But what the man pulled out instead was just a pack of cigarettes.

"You got a light?" he asked. "Think I dropped mine."

"Oh!" said Andrew, both surprised and relieved. "Sorry, I…uh…I don't smoke."

"Prob'ly a good idea, bad habit," said the man. "Anyway, you have a pleasant evening."

"You t—"

Andrew's response and his relief were both cut short when—much to his horror—Haley turned and pounced on the man with a noise that could *not* have been human. Instantly, her fingers were tipped with razor-sharp claws that tore open the stranger's jacket and raked across his chest. He fell back on the ground and lay motionless. Haley turned to face Andrew and he was horrified when he saw the fangs in her mouth.

"Holy shit!"

"Hey, hey, easy," said Haley, holding out her hand as her fangs and claws receded. "Look, okay, yes, I'm a vampire."

"So…that's what this all was? You were just trying to lure me back to your place to *bite* me?"

"What the hell kind of attitude is that?" asked Haley. "Oh right, just because I'm a vampire, that *must* mean I'm going to kill you?"

"Well…yeah!"

Haley scoffed. "Believe it or not, I actually like you—well, *liked*. Before I found out what a racist you are."

"Hold on, you're actually *offended* by my reaction?" asked Andrew.

"You're a young white guy, wouldn't you be offended if I assumed you were a serial rapist?"

"That's…that's not even close to being the same thing!"

"And after I saved your life from that creep, who by the way had been following us ever since we left the bar," said Haley. "Y'know what, maybe you should just take your bigotry and go home."

Andrew's mouth hung open in disbelief. "This is… insane."

"Maybe next time you shouldn't judge people based on what you've seen in movies!"

Haley slammed the gate behind her and went into the building, leaving Andrew just standing out there alone. He looked down at the body and jumped, almost forgetting it was still there. "Great, now what?"

He turned back to the mouth of the alley and started walking towards it.

"Uhhh, goddammit!"

Andrew's body froze. That voice was the same as the guy he just saw Haley killed. Slowly, he turned around and saw the man get back to his feet. He looked down at his tattered jacket and sighed. Then he glanced at Andrew while gesturing to the jacket. "You believe this shit? Brand-new fuckin' jacket…"

"What the hell is happening?"

"Apologies for all that."

This was a new voice that came from above. Andrew looked up and saw a man perched on a nearby garage. He hopped off and landed flawlessly on the ground. He was tall and bald, dressed in a long coat.

"My associate over there was just supposed to follow you, not engage," said the new arrival.

"And who are you?" asked Andrew.

"My name is Belial," he said, then nodded to the other guy. "That's Erik."

"And how is Erik not...dead?"

"I'm a lycan, kid," said Erik. "Or, y'know, 'werewolf' if you wanna go with the normie description.'

Andrew's eyes went large at that. He turned to Belial. "So, does that mean you're *also* a...a..."

"A lycan? No. I'm just a demon," said Belial.

"Wh-what the hell is going on tonight?" asked Andrew.

"The vampire was just some bad luck," said Belial.

"Yeah, sorry about that, kid. I thought she was actually going to bite you, so that's why I stepped in," said Erik.

"So you guys are what? Monsters hunting monsters? Trying to protect humanity in an attempt to redeem yourselves or something?" asked Andrew.

"No, actually, we're here because you made a deal about six months ago," said Belial.

"This is about what I owe? So you're saying you're supernatural loan sharks?"

"Basically, yeah," said Erik.

"A service was performed for you. You were given six months to pay what you owe," said Belial. "I'm here to claim what's due."

Andrew sighed. "C'mon, man. Can't you just give me a little more time?"

Belial removed his gloved hands from his coat pockets and cracked his knuckles as his eyes flashed yellow. "Do I look like a patient hellspawn, Mr. Greene?"

Andrew sighed. "I mean…it's just…things are rough out there…"

"Perhaps you'd like to know what happens to deadbeats in Hell?" asked Belial. "I can show you, though I doubt you'll find it a pleasant experience."

Andrew sighed and took out his phone. "Okay, just give me the account details…"

Erik took out his own phone and walked over to Andrew. "I got you covered, kid. Let's settle this now and then you can go home."

"Yeah, yeah…"

As the two performed the digital transaction, Belial looked at the apartment building Haley had retreated into. Vampires looking for actual one-night stands, sorcerers performing spells on demand, demons and werewolves acting as loan sharks. This was definitely a unique world he'd found himself in.

"Okay, big guy, we're all set here. Andrew's gonna get himself home and probably jack off through tears to the soft, blue glow of his computer," said Erik.

"And my fee?" asked Belial.

"Already taken care of, deposited right in your account," said Erik.

"Right…my account…" Belial reached into his pocket for the phone. He was still uncomfortable with this human technology, but he was starting to learn.

"Oh, and I got a message from the boss," said Erik. "He said if you need more work, he'd be happy to toss it your way."

"Thank you," said Belial. "Out of curiosity, what kind of spell did Odysseus Black perform for the boy?"

Erik chuckled. "You won't believe this. Kid wanted a

few extra inches below the belt."

Belial cocked his brow. "Penis enlargement? That's what this was all about?"

Erik shrugged. "Normies, man. What can I tell ya? Anyway, so about that extra work?"

Belial sighed. "I suppose so."

"Your boss is okay with this, right?" asked Erik. "Mr. Black wouldn't want to piss off the Morningstar or nothin'."

"No, it's perfectly fine," said Belial. "The Morningstar is…laying low for the time being."

CHAPTER 2

The bright-red Miata tore down Lake Shore Drive. The convertible top was down and the driver smiled as he felt the wind blow through his dark hair. A black-gloved hand reached for the shifter and he moved to a higher gear and stepped harder on the gas pedal.

A scream came from the passenger seat. The driver looked at his companion, a young redhead in a short, black dress whose hands were clasped over her eyes. He peeled one of her hands away, looking back and forth between her and the road.

"Come on, Isabel. What good is it riding in a car like this if you're going to cower the whole time?" he asked.

"C-can't you slow down just a little bit, Luke?"

Lucifer chuckled at her response and turned his attention back to the road, keeping just one hand at the top of the wheel. "Relax. I know what I'm doing."

"Doesn't seem like it!"

"Give me a *little* credit, okay? I've been driving for a whole month."

"...what?"

Lucifer spoke louder so his voice would carry over the wind. "I said I've been driving for a whole month."

11

"I heard you, that was a 'what the hell are you talking about' kind of what! You only got your license last month?"

"License? Who said anything about a license?"

Isabel parted her index and middle finger to peer at Lucifer. "You don't have a driver's license?"

"I know, and yet I'm still doing such a great job," he said. "It's amazing what you can learn from YouTube and *Need For Speed*."

"You mean you learned how to drive from a damn *video game*?"

"You say that like it's a bad thing."

Isabel started screaming again, demanding that Lucifer stop the car. He sighed as he weaved through the lanes, passing the slower vehicles.

"Don't worry, we'll be at my place in a few minutes. Then we can have a drink by the fire."

A high-pitched wail caught Lucifer's attention. His eyes shifted up at the rear-view mirror, turning it to get a better view and saw flashing red and blue lights.

"Oh look, we have company," he said.

Isabel pulled her hand away and turned around in her seat. She breathed with relief. "Oh thank Christ."

Lucifer frowned at the expression.

Isabel turned to him. "So you're gonna pull over now, right?"

Lucifer glanced at her, then back at the mirror, and then once more at Isabel. The corners of his lips curved slightly upwards and Isabel felt a sense of dread in the pit of her stomach.

"Oh no…please don't tell me you're gonna do what I think you're gonna do…"

"I think our friend wants a race," said Lucifer.

"No, no, no! No, he certainly does *not*!"

"Consider it an act of kindness," said Lucifer. "A way for the boys in blue to keep their driving skills sharp."

"Luke, no, don't even think about iiiiiiii—!"

The last syllable stretched into a scream as Lucifer took one of the exit ramps. He sped through the red light, pulling hard to the left. The Miata skidded through the intersection, with other cars swerving to avoid him. Before even stopping, Lucifer shifted and hit the gas again, and then took another left to get back on Lake Shore Drive, but this time heading south.

To his credit, the officer managed to keep up, following Lucifer's trail. Lucifer smiled as he watched the car in his mirror. He was on the far inside lane and sidling up beside another car. Lucifer moved ahead of the car beside him, and then, at the last minute, swerved in front of the middle car and across all the lanes. The cop inadvertently pulled ahead and Lucifer dropped back, slowing down just enough to get behind the cop.

"Okay, you lost him, now can you pull over and *let me out*?"

"What, so soon? We're just getting started, my dear."

Lucifer moved back through traffic, getting closer to the cop. The officer was obviously still trying to find Lucifer up ahead, so Lucifer decided to make his presence known. He pulled into the lane beside the cop and moved his car so the two of them were neck and neck. The cop was on his radio and not even paying attention to his peripheral vision, so Lucifer got his attention by hitting the horn.

The cop looked over, first with surprise and the face instantly turned to anger. Lucifer just laughed and sped on and the chase began anew.

LUCIFER DAMNED

"Ohgodohgodohgod I'm gonna die!"

Isabel kept muttering those words *ad nauseam*. Lucifer made a sharp right on Jackson, then a left on Columbus. Buckingham Fountain was to his left and the cop still kept on following. Lucifer took another left on Balboa, and then returned to Lake Shore Drive, completing the loop around the fountain.

His foot went heavy on the gas, the only sounds he could hear over the roar of the engine being Isabel's continued protestations. But they had barely passed the fountain when Isabel suddenly took the initiative, reaching over and grabbing the wheel. She pulled hard to the right just as they came to an intersection.

The car swerved and Lucifer fought with her for control, finally wresting the wheel back and skidding to a stop right in front of the Chicago Yacht Club. The squad car screeched to a stop beside them and just as the officer was climbing out of the car, Isabel had already hopped out of the Miata and ran to throw her arms over him. The cop was stunned but obviously not protesting an attractive young woman thanking him while pressing her body up against him.

When Lucifer got out of the driver's seat, the cop instantly went back to business. He drew his gun on Lucifer and aimed it at him. "Down on the ground!"

Lucifer offered a meek smile as he raised his arms over his head. "Aren't you overreacting just a bit, Officer?"

"I said get your ass on the ground and I meant right fucking *now*!"

Lucifer looked down at the white suit he wore, then back at the cop. "Do I really have to? To be perfectly honest, this suit might be worth more than the car itself."

"Oh, *please* tell me you're refusing to cooperate…"

Lucifer sighed and knelt down on the asphalt, then laid on his stomach. "As you wish. But I'll need your badge number so I know where to send the dry-cleaning bill once we're finished here."

The cop came closer, his gun still pointed at Lucifer. He took one hand off the weapon and reached for the handcuffs on his belt, then put his knee on Lucifer's back and pulled his arms down to restrain them. The cop slapped both cuffs on, and then pulled Lucifer up by the collar of his jacket.

"Is this really necessary?" asked Lucifer. "I promised Isabel we'd go back to my place for a nightcap."

"Not after that little driving stunt, you *psycho*!" screamed Isabel.

"You *said* you wanted to see what the car could do," said Lucifer, then glanced over his shoulder at the cop. "Honestly, what would you do if you were in my situation?"

"I didn't mean race a damn cop!" Isabel protested.

"Miss, this'll probably go a lot smoother if you head on home," said the cop. "You got a phone? Someone you can call to pick you up?"

Isabel scoffed. "Fine, whatever. I'll be changing my number first thing tomorrow, too, Luke, so don't bother calling!"

Lucifer kept his eyes on Isabel as she walked down Monroe and back towards the city lights. He gave another glance over his shoulder at the cop. "There goes my plan for the night. You *do* realize I was hoping to have sex with her tonight, don't you? Now who am I supposed to sleep with? You?"

"You're not going anywhere."

"I mean, no offense, it's not that I'm not tempted. You're certainly a handsome enough guy," said Lucifer. "But I have this thing about authority figures."

"Shut up, you're under arrest," said the cop.

"Am I?" asked Lucifer. "And you're sure this isn't some sort of sex thing?"

The cop tightened the cuffs and Lucifer felt the metal press into his wrists.

"Yeah, I'm sure," he said.

Lucifer was taken into custody after that incident for reckless driving and driving without a license. The car was impounded and his belongings were confiscated. At the station, they put him in lock-up for the night.

While most would be devastated by the turn of events or questioning the choices they'd made, Lucifer was oddly satisfied with the way things had transpired. He laid down across one of the benches in the large holding cell and rested his head on his hands, elbows out to the sides.

He was alone in the cell, but not for long. Within an hour or so, another detainee was brought in. The boy couldn't have been more than seventeen or so, and as soon as he sat on the bench, his bent legs started shaking, knees moving up and down repeatedly.

"Maybe lay off the coffee, kid," said Lucifer.

The kid looked at the man in the white suit, surprised to see someone dressed like that in a place like this. "Yeah, and why'd they arrest you? Catch you picking up a prostitute?"

"I was racing a Miata down LSD. When a cop tried to pull me over, I gave him a chase," said Lucifer. "I was caught and turns out you need a license to drive in Chicago. Who knew?"

The kid stared in disbelief for a few moments and then burst out into a chuckle. "If you didn't have a license, why didn't you drive slower?"

"Where's the fun in that?" Lucifer sat up on the bench and faced the kid. "What's your name?"

"Jimmy," he said. "How 'bout you?"

Lucifer smirked. "Just call me Luke." He took a breath, the satisfaction on his face obvious.

"What're you so happy about?" asked Jimmy. "In case you didn't notice, we're in prison."

"No, we're in jail, there's a difference," said Lucifer. "Besides, this is just temporary."

"Temporary or not, I'm gonna catch hell for this…"

Lucifer's laughter caught Jimmy by surprise. He gave the odd man a stare that held a mixture of curiosity and contempt. "What's so funny?"

"The idea that this is anything close to Hell." Lucifer's laughter faded and he waved a dismissive hand. "It's nothing. Just kind of an inside joke, I don't think you'd understand."

"Not so funny for me. My dad's gonna beat the shit outta me when he picks me up."

"And what is it you were doing?" asked Lucifer.

"Me an' some buddies went to this overpass and were tagging it. Nobody goes there, so we thought it'd be no problem. Then this cop shows up and grabs me."

"And your friends?"

"They bolted."

"First sign of trouble and they run," said Lucifer. "I had some experience with that. A very long time ago."

"Yeah? What happened?"

Lucifer took a breath and leaned forward, resting his arms on his thighs and steepling his fingers together.

"It's ancient history now, but there was a time, long ago, when I had learned an uncomfortable truth about my…family, I guess you could say."

"What do you mean by that? They weren't really your family? You adopted or something?"

"No, it's just…" Lucifer let out a breath as he tried to think of an easy way to explain it. "I was raised in a cult."

"No way. You mean like some kinda Heaven's Gate shit or something?"

"Yeah, something like that. Just without the mass suicide," said Lucifer. "Anyway, I learned the truth—that we'd been lied to all our lives. And I tried to tell my brother about it."

"Guessin' he liked the taste of the Kool-Aid?"

"That's one way of putting it," said Lucifer. "He turned on me, had me expelled from my home, and we haven't spoken since."

"Anyone have your back?"

"There were some, but not the ones I truly cared about," said Lucifer. "I lost my brother and I lost the woman I—a woman who was very special to me."

"She was part of this cult stuff, too?"

Lucifer nodded. "Indeed she was."

"So you haven't talked to your brother. What about her?"

"We've been in contact," said Lucifer. "Though seems each time we speak, things only seem to get worse. One step forward, two steps back."

"Maybe you gotta just move on then."

"Maybe you're right. It's something I'm trying to do now actually—leave all that in the past and move forward with my life as it is now." Lucifer looked across at Jimmy. "Might be something you should consider as well."

"Huh? When did this become about me?"

Lucifer shrugged. "You had people you thought you could count on and they turned their backs on you. Might be time to re-evaluate some of your relationships and where your life's going."

Jimmy frowned. "I dunno. I mean, not like I was all that keen on doing it in the first place. But at the same time…"

"You wanted to be one of the gang," said Lucifer. "Trust me, I understand that temptation. But the wonderful thing about freedom is you have a choice to follow your own instincts. Might be time to consider what *you* want instead of what some friends who bail at the first sign of trouble want."

The outer door to the cell block opened. A uniformed officer entered and walked over to the cell door. He opened it while staring at Lucifer. "Looks like you made bail."

"Well, fancy that."

Lucifer rose off the bench. Before he went to the cell door, he walked over to Jimmy and held out his hand. Jimmy looked up at the hand and into Lucifer's eyes. For the first time, the teen noticed how strange the odd man's eyes were—a kind of pale, faded yellow.

"Do yourself a favor and don't mess around with guys who are going to run out on you," said Lucifer. "Stick to your values and trust in those who truly have your back."

"You sayin' that for me or for yourself?" asked Jimmy.

Lucifer shrugged. "Maybe both of us."

"All right, I'll try." Jimmy shook Lucifer's hand.

Lucifer gave him a parting smile and then walked out of the cell. The officer locked the door and led him from the block over to a gated booth where an officer inside produced Lucifer's valuables and some forms on a clipboard. After signing for his belongings, the officer escorted Lucifer to a waiting room where Belial was waiting.

"You've made bail, but you've gotta show up at your court date," said the officer. "Failure to appear will result in a warrant being issued for your arrest."

"Understood," said Lucifer and he took the court documents provided by the officer. He left the officer's side and walked over to Belial, whose face remained stoic.

The two left the station in silence and went out to the parking lot. A car pulled up to the curb and Belial opened the door for Lucifer, who climbed into the car first. Belial followed, sliding into the seat next to him.

"Thank you, Erik," said Belial.

"Why did you come by car?" asked Lucifer.

"I was with Erik when I got your call. He felt it was best if he drive me. Might look suspicious if we walk out of the station and duck into an alley to teleport away," said Belial.

"Good thinking," said Lucifer. "And you, Erik? What's your business?"

"I work for Mr. Black, sir," said Erik from the driver's seat.

"Ah, right." Lucifer leaned back against the seat cushions and glanced in Belial's directions. "You're still running errands for Odysseus?"

Belial nodded. "The human world requires currency. So long as you remain powerless, we must earn some."

"There are other ways, you know," said Lucifer. "You could always knock over a bank."

"I'd prefer something lower profile," said Belial.

The rest of the drive was silent. Eventually, Erik pulled up to the large mansion in Evanston's Lakeshore Historic District. Lucifer got out of the car first and went to the front door. He started to unlock it, then noticed Belial was still standing by the driver's side door, speaking with Erik. But without access to the heightened senses his powers once granted him, Lucifer had no way of knowing what the two were discussing.

Eventually, the conversation finished and Belial joined Lucifer at the door. The demon said nothing as Lucifer opened the door and let them both in.

"What, no lecture after bailing me out, Dad?" asked Lucifer by way of a joke.

Belial removed his trench coat and hung it in the closet. He ascended the staircase without another word. Lucifer just watched him go and then went into the library to fix himself a drink.

Although Belial seemed to have a chip on his shoulder over the past few weeks, Lucifer still enjoyed this new arrangement he'd found for himself. Yes, he was powerless. But for the first time in his entire life, he felt truly free. And that was worth whatever silent treatment his right-hand demon would give him.

CHAPTER 3

After his eyes slowly opened, Lucifer sat up in bed and reached across to the clock on the nightstand. The time was just past noon. He slid his legs over the edge of the mattress and climbed out of bed. Lucifer went to the door and removed the red silk robe from the hook on the back. After tying the belt, he went out into the hall and started to walk towards the staircase.

The door to Belial's room was open and he stopped to glance inside. There was nothing in there other than a chest of drawers and a twin bed, which was immaculately made. Otherwise, the room was extremely Spartan. Lucifer went on down the stairs and called out Belial's name, but received no response. The house was empty.

Belial must have woken early—or at least earlier than noon—and already gone out. Presumably on another job for Odysseus Black. Lucifer did feel a tinge of guilt that Belial was working almost non-stop for the sorcerer, but it also seemed that the demon wanted to keep himself busy. And it wasn't as if Lucifer gave Belial much to do lately.

Lucifer made himself a pot of coffee and once it was ready, took a steaming cup out to the pool deck. He shivered in the cool breeze, wearing nothing other than the robe. Before he lost his powers, he was largely immune to the elements. But now that he was human, Lucifer experienced an odd sort of thrill by feeling the sting of the wind against his skin.

He sipped his coffee and reached into the pocket of the robe for his phone. Lucifer leaned against the deck's bannister and scrolled through the morning headlines. Before, he would be concerned with finding some sign of another of the Cocytus escapees. Now, he didn't have to worry about that. All he had to do was relax and enjoy his life.

The headlines didn't spark anything of note. Lucifer wondered what he should do for the day. There was the matter of the impending court date and once the police learned that the Miata had actually been stolen, it would be another charge. Lucifer imagined he could talk to Mara or Odysseus for a favor to get that matter taken care of. Both knew more than their fare share of crooked lawyers.

Lucifer wondered if he should perhaps find a way to thank Barbatos for being the instrument that led to the loss of his powers. Though that would be difficult, what with the demon now being a prisoner of one of the most feared loa in all creation. But he was surprisingly grateful nonetheless. Without his powers, he no longer had any responsibilities to concern himself with. And he could simply do what he'd intended to do since abdicating Hell's throne in the first place—enjoy retirement.

As the former ruler of Hell and a fallen angel, plus with an archdemon as a bodyguard, Lucifer hadn't put much thought into home security. There were no motion detectors, surveillance cameras, nor even a simple alarm on his home. Even since becoming human, Lucifer didn't even consider them.

It was an oversight that this day would make him regret.

A small, metal, cylindrical device landed on the deck, just a few feet away from Lucifer. The sound drew his attention, but before he could have a chance to closely examine it, the device released a thick cloud of smoke. Lucifer started coughing and tried to wave the smoke away to clear a path back to the house.

He went in through the patio door and closed them quickly to keep the smoke out, though some followed it inside. Lucifer's coughing continued without pause, though. He bent over the kitchen table, one hand braced against its surface, the other cupping his mouth as he hacked and coughed.

Between spurts, Lucifer heard a noise. He looked up and saw movement in the adjoining library. His powers once enabled him to weave weapons from the hellfire burning within him, so that meant there was no need to keep any physical weapons in his home. Another gross oversight.

Lucifer, still coughing, went to the kitchen counter. Mounted on the wall was a magnetic knife block. He reached for the butcher knife and pulled it free from the powerful magnet. It wasn't a hellfire sword, but it would have to do.

He bent down and walked over to the door leading to the library. The door was open and Lucifer peered through the opening. A man was inside, wearing a balaclava that covered his entire face, save for his eyes. He wore a leather jacket and jeans, and his the leather-gloved hands held a silver revolver.

There was a wide open space between the door and the

sofa. Lucifer watched the intruder, waiting for his back to turn just long enough so he could make it to the couch. The man looked away from Lucifer and that was when he made his move. He stayed low and quickly but quietly rushed across the gap.

Lucifer got down behind the sofa, his heart pounding hard against his chest. He went to the far end and peered around the corner. If he could get behind the guy, he could ambush him and cut his throat. Then that would be it.

"Ham!" the intruder suddenly called out. "The library's clear!"

"Goddammit!" came another voice. So there were at least two.

Lucifer peered around and saw another guy come into the room. He was larger than his partner, but also wearing the same style of clothes—leather jacket, jeans, and a balaclava.

"You're not supposed to use my name, Shem, you idiot!" said Ham.

"And *you* know you're not supposed to use the Lord's name in vain!" said the smaller one, who was obviously Shem. "Plus you just used *my* name!"

"That's because *you* used my name *first*! So if my cover's blown, so's yours! That's what's fair."

Lucifer sighed as he listened to them bicker. *Great, I'm about to be killed by Heckle and Jeckle.*

"Look, we've got a job to do. You know how important this is," said Shem. "If we do this right, Father will know we've got what it takes and let us back into the guild."

"*I know that*! Why do you keep explaining things to me over and over again? Just because I'm the big one doesn't make me the dumb one," said Ham.

"I never said you were dumb, I just know that some-times you—"

"Wait." Ham covered Shem's mouth with his hand. "Did you check that couch?"

Lucifer saw Ham's gaze moving in his direction and he slid back behind the sofa. He held the butcher's knife in a reverse-grip.

"He's not hiding *in* the couch, Ham."

"Not *in* the couch, you moron. *Behind* it." Ham moved away from Shem and reached behind his back to draw an ornate dagger from its sheath. "And you treat me like *I'm* the dumb one…unbelievable…"

Lucifer listened for the footsteps, and stared at the floor. Ham's shadow loomed closer, growing larger. This was it, this was the moment. Lucifer jumped up and lashed out with the butcher knife.

And all he cut was empty air.

"That…wasn't how I expected it to go…" muttered Lucifer.

Ham smiled and waved the dagger. It had a gold hilt and a long cross-guard, which made it reminiscent of a crucifix. He thrust forward and Lucifer just barely jumped back to avoid the blade. Lucifer threw the knife, but Ham ducked and it harmlessly flew over his head.

"Time to die, Satan!" shouted Ham as he charged at the Morningstar.

Lucifer was near the liquor cabinet. He picked up a bottle of gin and smashed it on Ham's face right as he came within reach. Ham was startled and stumbled and fell face-first on the ground.

"That was my brother!" shouted Shem and opened fire.

Lucifer jumped behind the sofa and rolled, waiting

as Shem fired. It was a revolver, so Lucifer counted. Once he reached the final round, the gun clicked on the empty chamber.

"Oh poop, time-out," said Shem as he fumbled to open the chamber and reload the gun.

Lucifer didn't honor the time-out. He stood and leapt over the sofa, then darted towards Shem. The smaller brother looked up in surprise.

"No fair, I called a time-out!" shouted Shem just as Lucifer barreled into him, putting all his weight into a shoulder-strike. Shem was thrown back into the wall and Lucifer went into the foyer.

In the driveway was a minivan that looked to be several years old and not in the best condition. Lucifer went to the driver's seat and opened the door. It was unlocked and the keys were still in the ignition.

"First bit of luck today," said Lucifer as he turned the key. The engine puttered and rattled. Lucifer turned the car off and tried again, stepping on the gas a few times. The engine still wasn't quite ready to reward him. "Come on, come on…"

Lucifer glanced behind the seats and saw several weapons stacked up in the van. He reached over and picked up a shotgun. Pointing it out the open car window, Lucifer aimed at his front door. Shem appeared in the doorway and raised the revolver. Lucifer pulled the trigger and Shem ducked, the buckshot taking out several chunks of the wood in the frame.

"I'll definitely be billing them for that." Lucifer tried the ignition again and this time, the car started. He laughed and shifted into reverse, looking over his shoulder as he backed out into the street.

"That's our van! This isn't how it's supposed to happen!" Shem shouted as he ran after the car.

Lucifer ignored the protests and shifted into drive, then sped down the street towards Chicago. Although "speed" was probably not the best use of words—the van didn't exactly have a whole lot of pick-up.

As he merged onto Lake Shore Drive and headed into the city, Lucifer thought about the odd incident. Those two definitely weren't demons and they certainly didn't seem skilled enough to be part of any sort of organized outfit. It wasn't likely they were simple thieves, either—they were after him.

Lucifer remembered that Shem mentioned something about their father and a guild. He would have to find out more about those two feckless, would-be hitmen. And for that, he would need to consult some help. Someone who could possibly know something about this and who would provide assistance without any strings attached.

There was only one person in the city who fit both those criteria.

CHAPTER 4

Miraculously, Lucifer had somehow managed to get the rickety van he stole from Shem and Ham all the way from Evanston to the city. He parked it on Rush Street in front of a fire hydrant and climbed out, leaving the keys in the ignition. He was still dressed only in his silk robe and a pair of slippers.

A nearby pedestrian called out to the Morningstar. "Hey Hef, you'd better move your car."

"Why?" asked Lucifer.

"Because the city's gonna tow it if you leave it there."

Lucifer shrugged. "Not my car anyway."

He whistled as he crossed the street, waving greetings to the people who were stunned to see a man walking the streets in nothing but a robe. Lust was his destination—on the surface, it was a fashionable night club. But beneath that thin veneer, it was a gathering place for the supernatural elements of Chicago. At one time it was run by Asmodeus, who—after a run-in with Luther Cross—ended up imprisoned in Cocytus. Now it was under the control of Asmodeus's former paramour, Lilith. She remained in Hell, but left a trusted lieutenant to watch over her operations on Earth.

The club itself wouldn't open for business until around nine or ten at night. But Lucifer was one of the few aware of the apartment above the club where the manager resided. And also knew of the rear entrance.

He walked up the staircase that led to the sole room at the top of the building. Lucifer pushed the button and waited. After a few moments, there was no answer. Lucifer rang the bell a second time. Just as he was about to go for the hat-trick, the door finally opened.

"I will personally rip every tooth out of your goddamn skull and use them to decorate my bathroom," said the demon with fiery red hair and wearing sweat pants and a black T-shirt with "SATANIC PANIC" emblazoned on the front.

"Good morning to you as well, Mara," said Lucifer, his arms folded over his chest. "Or should I say 'good afternoon'?"

Mara's yellow eyes nearly bulged out of her skull when she saw who her visitor was. She immediately dropped down to her knees in supplication. "Forgive my manner, My Lord. I-I didn't realize it was you."

"Stand up, stop embarrassing yourself," said Lucifer as he walked past Mara and into her apartment. "You know how I hate that."

Mara rose to her feet and closed the door. "I'm sorry, it's been a while since I've seen you."

"Yes, I've been a bit busy as of late," said Lucifer.

Mara stared at his clothing—or rather, lack thereof. Lucifer could feel her eyes crawling over him.

"Go on, you know you want to ask," he said.

Mara was uncharacteristically bashful, her cheeks actually turning red as she looked down. Slowly, she raised her chin, her eyes still moving from side to side as if she were trying to avoid looking directly at Lucifer. This routine went on for a few moments before finally, she addressed the elephant in the room.

"Why…why are you wearing a robe?"

"Because I had just woken up. I made myself some coffee, went out to the deck, and just enjoyed the slow start to my day," he began. "And then I was suddenly attacked."

Mara's reticence turned into shock. "What? Who would dare attack you?"

"Oh, I imagine lots would dare," said Lucifer. "But in this instance, it was two humans. I got the sense they were some sort of demon hunters. And I thought who better to go to for information than the queen of the supernatural underworld."

Mara looked away again with a smile forcing its way onto her face. "I'm hardly any sort of queen…just keep things in order for my mistress. More of a regent, really."

"Whatever you choose to call yourself, you're my best source of information on this," said Lucifer.

"Of course, I'd be happy to help you in any way I can. But…there's one thing I'm still not so clear on."

"What's that?" asked Lucifer.

"These men attacked you, you dispatched them, and then you came here," she said. "So…I still don't understand the robe."

Lucifer frowned. "I…actually didn't—the hunters are still alive."

"Why would you leave them a—oh, I see," said Mara, believing she'd discovered some master plan. "You left them alive as a warning. Probably maimed them terribly so other hunters would know not to come after the Morningstar."

Lucifer's lips pursed and stretched as he tried to push himself to say the words he didn't want to say. "No. I…had to escape. In their beat-up old van. And so I didn't have time to get dressed."

Mara looked concerned. "Do you think it might have been Heaven attacking you? Because I do know about this one time when an angel imbued his followers with his own power. Could be that Uriel has decided to make a move against you."

"They weren't imbued with anything," said Lucifer. "They were just normal demon hunters."

"They must have been extremely formidable then. I know the Vatican employs highly trained assassins. And there's also the Sons of Solomon and some very dangerous independent guilds…"

Lucifer's lips tightened. He walked over to a liquor cabinet and opened it, helping himself to a bottle of bourbon. Without even asking, Lucifer removed the top and started drinking straight from the bottle.

"…sir?" asked Mara.

"It was two of them. Their names were Shem and Ham," said Lucifer. "And they were utterly incompetent."

Mara looked as if Lucifer had just spoken gibberish to her. "I don't understand…if they were so incompetent, then why did you have to escape from them? Is this some sort of ploy to lure them into a false sense of security?"

"It's no damn ploy!" Lucifer shouted. He closed his eyes and took a breath to calm himself. "I'm sorry. What I mean is I have…a situation."

"…situation?"

"I inadvertently seem to have burned out my powers. At first, I thought it would be temporary. But now, it seems as if it's permanent," said Lucifer. "And without my powers, I'm just…"

"Human," said Mara in disbelief. "When did this happen?"

"About a month or so ago. Barbatos was one of the Cocytus escapees and I lost my powers dealing with that situation," said Lucifer. "Since then, I've been left stripped, so to speak. No psychometry, not even a spark of hellfire, I can't even use basic magic without some sort of intermediary."

"If this happened a month ago, then how come I'm just hearing about it now?" asked Mara.

Lucifer took another swig from the bottle and collapsed on Mara's couch. "I didn't want to broadcast it for obvious reasons. Enough people already know that the Devil is on Earth. If they knew he was powerless as well…"

"There would be waves of enemies out to kill you," said Mara. "So that begs the question—how did these two learn about it?"

Lucifer took another drink. All this time, his assumption was that Shem and Ham simply attempted a foolhardy assault and had no knowledge of his current state. They certainly seemed stupid enough to think they could face the power of the Morningstar on their own. But what if Mara had a point—what if someone had informed them of his current state?

"That's a very good question," said Lucifer.

"What do you know about them?"

"They were brothers, and they also mentioned something about their father's guild…"

"And you said their names were Shem and Ham?"

Lucifer nodded. "In the Bible, Noah had two sons named Shem and Ham."

"Their father must run one of those independent guilds. A number of them exist across the world, quite a few here in America. More often than not, they tend to be ultra-zealous religious militias. Not too many operating in Chicago, they tend to exist in more rural areas," said Mara.

"I'd imagine they'd face significant pushback from the different factions out here," said Lucifer.

"That's before you consider the larger, more organized groups, like the Vatican, the Sons of Solomon…"

"And OSIRIS," said Lucifer.

Mara raised an eyebrow. "What's that?"

"Seems Uncle Sam is getting involved in supernatural affairs as well," said Lucifer. "Though they don't seem particularly zealous, more concerned with maintaining order. Two of their agents actually helped Belial and I shut down Barbatos."

"Do they know about your powers?" asked Mara.

Lucifer looked up at her. "You think they're responsible for siccing the Wonder Twins on me?"

Mara shrugged. "Is it that outside the realm of possibility? Wouldn't be the first time the US government used proxies to deal with their dirty work."

"That's true…" muttered Lucifer. "You have a phone I can borrow? I need to reach Belial and I dropped mine during the escape. I'd like to get back to the house now and could use his help."

"Of course. But I'll go back there with you right now, no need to wait for Belial," said Mara. "He's not the only one indebted to you."

"That would be helpful," said Lucifer. He looked down

at his robe. "And I don't suppose you have any clothes in my size…?"

Mara's eyes burned bright yellow as she waved her hands. Energy crackled around Lucifer's body, shifting the robe until it transformed into a silk red suit with a black, open-collared shirt. Lucifer examined the new clothing and gave a smile of satisfaction.

"Much better," he said. "Although I will need you to turn this back into a robe later."

"I will. Although there's a bigger problem," said Mara. "Now that these two know, who's to say how many others will find out? You're going to have a target on your back. Do you know of a way to restore your powers?"

Lucifer paused. Then he just stood from the couch, buttoned the jacket, and walked past Mara towards the front door. "I'm afraid I haven't come up with anything just yet."

CHAPTER 5

Not only did Lucifer leave the van in a place it would definitely be towed, but the stockpile of weapons inside would definitely give the police reason to investigate further. And now that Mara was with him, Lucifer had no need of the van for transportation purposes—her wings could teleport them both instantly to Lucifer's front door.

They materialized about a block away just in case Shem and Ham were still lurking around. Didn't seem likely as strategy certainly wasn't their strong suit, but it was best to take precautions so as not to be caught unawares. The two of them walked the short distance to Lucifer's home.

The front door was left open. Mara took the lead and once inside the foyer, she conjured a hellfire sword in her hands. The library was to the left of the foyer and she checked inside there, first. Some books had been removed from the shelves, but they were left discarded on the floor. There was broken glass in a puddle of gin from Lucifer's attack on Ham, as well as the butcher knife Lucifer had thrown in the fight.

Mara moved through the library and into the kitchen. Also empty and not much of note in there. She continued forward, but as she came closer to the living room, she could sense another presence. Mara held up her hand, signaling for Lucifer to stay back. She gripped her sword with both hands and pushed open the sliding door with her foot.

She charged in the living room and raised the sword, prepared to bring it down on the remaining intruder. But she met with sudden resistance in the form of another flaming sword. Mara locked eyes with the intruder and her face carried a hint of surprise.

Mara's sword vanished, the hellfire retreating back into her arms. The 'intruder' did the same as well, just as Lucifer entered the room behind Mara. He too was surprised to see the third person, though he probably shouldn't have been.

"Belial?" asked Lucifer. "What are you doing here?"

"I live here," said Belial.

"We tried to contact you, but we didn't get an answer," said Mara.

"I got your message and I came right over," said Belial. "I hoped to catch the would-be assassins before they managed to escape."

"And did you?" asked Lucifer.

Belial shook his head. "They were gone by the time I arrived. It seems they tried searching for some useful information, but I didn't see any books unaccounted for."

"No, my guess is they saw that the books weren't in whatever idiot variant of English they speak, and so they just left them behind," said Lucifer. "Or perhaps it was the lack of pictures that put them off."

"Whatever the case, we need to press on ahead," said Belial.

"Agreed," said Lucifer. "I didn't find my phone, so my guess is they must have taken it, thinking they could get some information off it. Not only are they likely too stupid to access anything on the device, but I'll bet they didn't even think about disabling the GPS. We can find them that way and then I can learn more about why they came for me."

Belial didn't say anything at first. Instead, he just stared at Lucifer. The Morningstar quickly got the impression that his loyal bodyguard had a very different idea in mind for how to deal with the situation.

"Do you…disagree?" asked Lucifer.

"Don't you think there's something else we should focus on first?" asked Belial.

"Like what?"

"It's dangerous for you to go after them in your current state. The priority should be restoring your powers," said Belial.

"It would definitely be ideal, but we can't wait around for that," said Mara. "Probably won't take long before they realize they can't do anything with the Morningstar's phone. And at that point, they'll probably toss it and head off into hiding. Wasting precious lead time to research a way for Lucifer to restore his powers—"

Belial cut her off, holding up his hand. "Hold on, what are you saying? What needs to be researched?"

Mara blinked a few times. "How to restore his powers. So far, we don't know what can be done—"

"Yes, we do," said Belial. "Lucifer's powers are tied to Hell. What we need to do is return there and then he can be restored. Who told you—"

Belial stopped himself and looked at Lucifer. He let out a huff. "Of course, now I see."

Lucifer narrowed his eyes at his companion. "Is there

something you want to say?"

Belial shook his head and began walking from the living room back to the foyer. "I should go. I have work to do."

"Somehow I doubt that Odysseus Black is sending you out on a job in the afternoon," said Lucifer, walking after the demon. "If there's something you want to say to me, then you may as well just say it."

Belial was standing by the front door in the foyer. He stopped and turned around. "I have no desire to speak my mind."

"Isn't that what we fought for in the first place? Isn't that why we rebelled? For the freedom to speak our minds?" asked Lucifer.

Belial had the door open and was about to walk through it when Lucifer called him out. He sighed and slammed the door shut, then turned to face the being he had once called his lord and master.

"Are you certain you wish to hear my words?" he asked.

Lucifer stood tall, raising his chin up to look the taller demon directly in the eyes. "I live my life according to my values, Belial. Speak freely."

"Very well." Belial folded his arms over his chest and stared down at Lucifer. "You're a coward."

A quick shake of his head signaled how taken aback Lucifer was by the response. "I beg your pardon?"

Mara stepped closer to Belial. "You're out of line, demon. This is the Morningstar you're talking to! The only one who had the courage to stand up to the Divine Choir!"

"All the more reason why I myself feel just how deep that accusation stings," said Belial. "But Lucifer asked for my honest opinion. Or would he rather I keep quiet unless it's in support of him?"

Lucifer's teeth were gritted behind his lips. His fingers tightened, threatening to curl into fists. But he calmed himself and stretched out his hands. His jaw loosened and he spoke.

"No, Mara. I believe I stand for freedom, and so I need to actually live up to that promise," he said. "Belial has every right to his opinion, just as I have every right to disagree with him."

"Shall we examine the evidence?" asked Belial. "You know what you need to do in order to restore your powers. And this incident has shown that you are vulnerable. Others are already aware of your situation. In time, the people who know the truth will simply increase. It won't be long before enemies are banging down your door."

Mara sighed and looked down. It took her a few moments before she turned her gaze to Lucifer. "I hate to take sides against you, but Belial does make a convincing argument. These two were just the beginning. Destroying them won't make a bit of difference—more will still come."

Lucifer turned his back on the pair. "All I ever wanted was the freedom to satisfy my curiosity. To discover new things about the universe and about our nature. All I wanted to do was to learn. But at every turn, I've been denied that chance. I was convinced to become the leader of a revolt. I was coerced into sitting on the throne of Hell. Even after my abdication, I was dragged back into these old conflicts to capture the Cocytus escapees.

"But now? My responsibility for all that is gone. I'm just a human and the only responsibility I have is to myself." Lucifer turned and faced the pair once again. "And yet, I still find others trying to push me back. To deny me the only thing I've ever truly wanted."

"I would wish nothing more than for you to have your heart's desire," said Belial. "But what good is pursuing that desire if you're destroyed before you can enjoy it?"

"That's a possibility," said Lucifer. "You're right, Belial. I could very well be killed tomorrow. If not by Shem and Ham, then maybe by someone else—a more-skilled hunter, a demon wanting to make a name for themselves, an angel. Or I might just slip in the shower and break my neck. But if I die, at least I'll go out pursuing the life I wanted. And that's a sacrifice I'm willing to make."

"I don't know if you realize what you're saying," said Mara.

"Of course I know, Mara. No need to patronize me," said Lucifer. "I'm tired of being some pawn on a cosmic chessboard. If I have to throw down my life to escape that cycle, then that's what I'll do."

He folded his arms in defiance and stared the two demons down. "Now the two of you have a choice. Either you can accept my decision and help me find these two assholes, or you can get the hell out of my house. What's your choice?"

Mara and Belial exchanged glances with each other as a means of silent communication. Neither spoke for several minutes, weighing the choice Lucifer had thrown at their feet. Mara was the one to speak first.

"I'll side with the Morningstar," she said. "Always."

Lucifer nodded in her direction. "Thank you, Mara." He then looked to Belial. "And you?"

Belial lowered his arms to the side. He met Lucifer's gaze with his own, but he didn't open his mouth to speak. Rather than engage further, Belial simply turned his back and walked out the front door without a single word.

CHAPTER 6

After Belial left without a word, Lucifer began the process of tracking down his would-be assassins. Just as expected, they weren't clever enough to realize that the GPS in his phone could be tracked and all Lucifer had to do to find it was log in through the internet and the location was displayed easily on a map.

"They're at a motel outside the city," said Lucifer as he slid his chair back from the desk where the laptop rested. "Whatever organization they're with, it looks like they don't spring for the best accommodations."

Mara came up behind him and looked at the monitor from over his shoulder. "Or maybe they're operating without sanction."

"Could be," said Lucifer. "They did mention something about impressing their father."

"How should we proceed?" asked Mara. "Do you want me to kill them or simply maim them?"

"Neither, I'm going with you," said Lucifer. "I want to find out what exactly they know and how they know it."

"But without your powers, are you sure you want to put yourself in danger?"

"Before, they caught me unawares and without back-up. But now, I have you and the element of surprise on my side. I'm fairly confident you can take care of them both. Just remember to leave them alive so I can still question them."

"Understood. So shall we go?" she asked.

Lucifer stood from the desk and stepped beside her. "You have the location pinpointed?"

She gave a nod. "Within a reasonable amount of distance."

Mara's eyes began to crackle and light started pouring forth from her back. Wings made of energy emerged and once they reached their full span, they became leathery, bat-like flesh. The demonic wings enveloped both her and Lucifer and then started glowing as they did before. The light flashed and they were gone, only to re-materialize on the shoulder of an expressway offramp.

Mara unfurled her wings and they receded into her back. Lucifer took the first steps forward. Just past the ramp off the side of the road was a budget motel advertising free cable and wifi included with the rooms.

"All we know is that they're somewhere in here," said Lucifer. "We'll have to check with the front desk to get their room."

"Should we torture the information out?" asked Mara.

Lucifer gave her a disgusted look. "Not everything requires torture, Mara. Sometimes, you can get the information you need just by asking for it in the right way."

He started walking towards the motel entrance. Mara shrugged and said, "Sure, but where's the fun in that?"

She jogged to catch up to his side. The two of them walked across the parking lot, which was mostly empty, and went to the glass door with RECEPTION stamped across the front. Lucifer opened the door and walked in, Mara right behind him.

A man sat behind the desk, his back to the entrance. He was reclined in the chair, his feet propped up on a back counter and watching a small TV. Lucifer stepped up to the front counter and rang the bell. The man was startled by the sound and nearly fell out of the chair. He spun the chair around to face the two surprise guests. His face was lined with wrinkles and he had a beard that was pure white.

"Sorry, didn't hear you come in," he said. "What can I do you for? You folks need a room?"

"As a matter of fact, no," said Lucifer. "We're actually here about two of your guests. One is tall and broad. The other is shorter and thin. They're brothers, both seem sort of clueless."

"I'm sorry, but I can't tell you anything about our guests," he said. "We guarantee privacy and discretion."

Lucifer gave a glance around the front office. "Yes, I'm sure some of your guests would have an appreciation for that. But I don't think you quite grasp the severity of the situation. You see, these two gentlemen are dangerous individuals and I don't think you want to get mixed up with them."

"Listen, Mister, I can appreciate your need to find these two. But unless you show me a badge and a warrant, then there's nothin' I can do for you."

Lucifer sighed. "I'd like to give you the opportunity to reconsider."

The manager just shook his head. "Sorry, but I can't budge on this. Discretion is our policy."

"Very well, just remember that I gave you the opportunity." Lucifer stepped away and glanced at Mara. "He's all yours."

The demon smiled as she stepped forward, her eyes beginning to burn like hot coals. The manager backed away from the front counter, but Mara jumped onto its surface. She reached out and grabbed him by his throat and raised his feet off the ground as if he weighed less than nothing. Her fiery eyes stared into his and he felt his pants beginning to dampen.

Mara threw him over the counter and right through the glass door. She hopped off the counter and stepped through the broken glass. The manager crawled on the pavement, the broken shards cutting into his skin as he did. He wasn't able to get very far before Mara picked him up by the scruff of his neck and threw him against the wall.

Before he could recover, she grabbed his throat and lifted him up, pressing him against the building. She flexed her free hand and a flaming dagger materialized in it, which she brought up to his face. Slowly, she waved the blade in front of him, his eyes wide and following the fiery trail as it went back and forth.

"Do you know how hellfire works, old man?" she asked. "You see, it's not like regular fire. That just burns your flesh. Those wounds can heal. But hellfire? Oh, that's a different story. You see, a hellfire blade, it doesn't just burn your skin—it sears your very soul. And it's a scar that will never fade. The memory of the pain it inflicts will remain vivid in your nightmares for eternity."

Lucifer peered through the broken door. "You heard what she said, friend. Are you sure you're willing to go through all that just to protect these boys?"

"Okay, okay!" he pleaded. "I'll tell you anythin' you

wanna know, just please call this psycho-bitch off!"

"Is that any way to talk to a lady?" asked Mara.

"I'm sorry! I'm just so scared, please, just put me down…Jesus Christ, I've got grandkids!"

"Mara, I think he's had enough," said Lucifer.

Mara gave Lucifer an incredulous look. "Really? Already?"

Lucifer nodded. Mara pouted, but released her grip and the manager fell to the ground. With a closing of her fist, Mara extinguished the hellfire dagger and then she stepped back to make room for Lucifer. He knelt down in front of the manager.

"So, you're willing to help us now?" he asked.

The manager gave repeated nods. Lucifer helped him to his feet and back into the office. The manager gingerly moved back behind the counter to check the computer records.

"By the way, I'm sorry about the door," said Lucifer. "Mara can get a little…overenthusiastic."

The manager didn't even acknowledge Lucifer's apology, just focused on his computer. "We had two guys like you described book a room last night. It's a double…room 19."

"There, now that wasn't so hard, was it?" asked Lucifer with a smile.

"If you're gonna kill them, could you…maybe do it somewhere else?" asked the manager.

Lucifer bowed. "You have my word." He stepped outside the office and met up with Mara once more. "That was a bit over-the-top, don't you think?"

"Was it?" asked Mara.

"Just a skosh," said Lucifer. He walked down the row

of rooms, counting past the numbers until they came to room 19. "Ah, here we are. Now remember, I *do* need them both alive."

Mara nodded and stepped up to the door. She swung her leg up and kicked it, breaking through the wood and rendering the lock useless. Inside, Shem fell off one of the twin beds and looked at the demon with fear.

"What the hell was that noise?" Ham emerged from the bathroom wearing nothing but a towel, shaving cream lathered over his face. Once he saw what had happened, he shouted, "Oh shit!"

"The Morningstar requests an audience," said Mara.

Shem scurried under the bed, and Mara bent over. She took hold of the frame and flipped the bed over onto its twin, then saw Shem lying on the ground with a revolver clutched in both hands. He pulled the trigger and the gun went off, striking Mara in her shoulder. She gritted her teeth at the pain she felt—an unusual amount of pain for a typical bullet-wound. But she noticed the engravings on the gun's barrel, meaning the weapon was one designed to ward off supernatural beings.

Ham charged forward and slammed into Mara. Taken by surprise and slightly weakened from Shem's gun, Mara was knocked off her feet and back out the door. Ham was on top of her and his fists managed to strike her face a few times. But Mara quickly recovered and Ham's fist stopped in mid-strike, mere inches from her face. He struggled against Mara's telekinetic hold on his fist, but slowly his arm changed direction. And when Mara released her hold, Ham ended up punching himself right in the face.

With a flick of her fingers, Mara's telekinesis threw Ham off her. He landed on his ass just outside the door.

Mara walked up to him and grabbed him by both ears, then slammed his head against the wall. Ham groaned and grunted with each strike, but he managed to hold on to consciousness.

That was until Mara drove her knee right into his face. She released her grip and Ham slumped to the ground, his face bruised and bloody and his eyes shut.

Mara stepped back inside the room, but had to duck out almost immediately once Shem fired another shot. She sighed and looked down at her hand. With her powers slightly weakened from that first shot, it took a little bit more effort for her to summon hellfire. But once she did, it appeared in the form of a small shotgun.

She turned into the room and immediately raised the gun, then fired it. The flaming hellfire shell exploded from the barrel and struck Shem right in the chest. The force of impact threw his rail-thin body against the wall and when he landed, it was face-down. Unconscious, just like his brother.

Mara picked up Shem and threw him over her shoulder. She exited the room and bent down to take hold of Ham's foot, then started dragging him behind her as she walked to meet up with Lucifer again.

"Taken care of," she said.

"Good, now just let me grab my phone and then we can get out of here." Lucifer casually strolled past the splintered door with his hands in his pockets. He looked at the spot where Shem's bed had been, but saw nothing on the ground there. Lucifer peeked under the twin beds that rested upon each other, still seeing nothing.

He went to the dresser and started opening drawers. One of them held a small collection of guns, knives, holy water, and other weapons. It seemed what Lucifer had found in their van was far from the extent of their arsenal. But also amidst the weapons was his phone. He picked it up, turned on the screen to ensure it was indeed his, and once he was satisfied, put it in his inner breast pocket.

"Everything settled?" asked Mara when Lucifer emerged to rejoin her.

Lucifer nodded. "Yes, I've got the phone. But the question is where should we take these two?"

"There's a basement in Lust. Asmodeus used to use it for just such an occasion," said Mara.

"Seems appropriate. Very well, then let's go there and find out just how these two little fail-sons stumbled on their information."

Lucifer glanced past Mara when he noticed the manager emerge from the front office to see what had happened. He looked at the room in horror, and then turned his attention to Lucifer and Mara.

"Don't worry!" said Lucifer as he waved. "They're still alive and we'll be getting out of your hair now."

Mara's wings emerged from her back and wrapped around all four of them. They vanished in a flash of light, leaving the manager standing alone in the parking lot.

"Now who's gonna clean all this shit up…?" he wondered.

CHAPTER 7

Referring to the area beneath Lust as a basement seemed like an understatement. To Lucifer, it looked more like a dungeon. There were shackles hanging from the walls, trays of sharp and blunt instruments, a shelf of chemicals, a collection of whips neatly coiled, and several other devices and instruments—the purposes of which Lucifer didn't exactly want to imagine. In addition, there were even some containment cells.

"You said Asmodeus used this room?" asked Lucifer.

Mara had already fastened the hanging shackles on the unconscious Shem and now she was doing the same to Ham. "Yeah. Seems he would use it when he wanted to get some information out of someone."

"And you've found use for it, too?"

"So far, I haven't really had much cause to use this place," said Mara. "Generally I don't torture for fun, I do it when I have a purpose."

"I find that hard to believe. You certainly seemed enthusiastic about the prospect earlier."

Mara gave a soft chuckle. "I never said I don't enjoy it. Just that when I do it, I want there to be a reason. Otherwise, it just doesn't give off that same rush, you know?"

"Not particularly. I never quite understood what it was the other demons loved so much about the act," said Lucifer as he explored some of the cutting instruments laid out on a tray. "To me, it just always seemed a bit excessive."

"And yet, here we are," said Mara.

"Oh, we're not going to torture them," said Lucifer.

Mara's jaw hung so low, it looked as if it had come unhinged. She blinked at the revelation a few times, trying to grasp what she'd just heard. "I'm sorry, you said we're *not* going to torture them?"

"No," said Lucifer. "You see, these two don't strike me as elite warriors or anything. I have a feeling all we'll need to do is provide them with some sufficient threats and they'll tell us everything I want to know."

"But…" Mara pouted.

"We're not here for you to indulge in your sadistic tendencies. We're here for information. And torture is hardly a reliable way to extract information."

Mara scoffed. "Well, *now* you tell me…"

They waited in silence until their prisoners woke. Ham was sufficiently angered once he realized he was shackled and immediately began to tire himself out in futile attempts at escape. He tried swinging his arms and legs as fiercely as he could in hope of either breaking open or sliding out of the restraints. This went on for several minutes before he tired himself out and ultimately was left pushing his back up against the wall and panting. Shem made a few attempts of his own, but he gave up on the effort a lot sooner than his brother.

"If you're both finished, might we move on to business?" asked Lucifer.

"Let me outta here and I'll show you what sort of business we'll conduct!" said Ham.

"That's a very optimistic worldview you have, Mr. Ham," said Lucifer. "But Mara already kicked your ass once. Are you really so eager for an encore?"

"I'll die fighting to eradicate you from existence, Satan!"

Lucifer clicked his tongue. "So droll. So clichéd. It's really just sad."

"Why'd you bring us here anyway? Gonna torture us or somethin'?" asked Shem.

Lucifer cocked his head in Mara's direction. "If she had her way, that's what we'd be doing. But I have other interests that take precedence. I'd like us to talk for a bit."

"You wanna have a chat?" asked Ham.

"Precisely. I'd like to learn more about you two fine gentlemen. For starters, just how exactly you came to this line of work."

"That's none of your business," said Ham.

"When you attacked me, Shem chided you for taking the Lord's name in vain. And your names are Biblical, so I'm going to assume you had a strict religious upbringing. You also mentioned your father's guild, plus the arsenal in your van suggests you have some connections," said Lucifer. "I'd like to know just what guild you're referring to."

"Why, so you can kill them yourself?" asked Ham. "I ain't tellin' you jack."

"How did you find out my location? Why did you assume you could wage an attack with just the two of you?" asked Lucifer.

"You're gonna have to torture me if you want me to talk," said Ham.

"That's right!" Shem chimed in. "Because no way are we gonna tell you about the Redeemers!"

Ham's face contorted in a combination of embarrassment and anger. "Shem, you fucking moron!"

"Redeemers, huh?" Lucifer moved from Ham over to Shem. "And who might the Redeemers be?"

"Uhh…I dunno what you're talkin' about," said Shem. "I've never heard of no Redeemers before. Maybe you're just hearing things."

"They're a fundamentalist militia," said Mara from her position leaning against the far wall. "If I'm not mistaken, they mostly operate in the southern area of the state."

"Good work, Shem," muttered Ham.

"We don't—I mean they don't operate in the southern area," said Shem, stammering to try to correct his error. "They're in…umm…Los Angeles! That's right, they moved out to LA 'cause of all the…the sin…an' demons…and…"

"Just shut up and stop embarrassing us," said Ham.

"If the Redeemers had not only known your location but your current state, there's no way they would have just sent these idiots," said Mara. "You'd have a full-blown attack force coming down on you."

"Which means only you two knew," said Lucifer, staring into Shem's eyes. The thin fundamentalist squirmed under his gaze, trying to look away. Lucifer grabbed his chin and forced him to look into his eyes. "So tell me, Shem. How did just the two of you come across this information?"

"Leave him alone," said Ham. "He's an idiot, he don't know nothin'."

"I know plenty!" said Shem. "The angel picked us because—"

"Dammit!" Ham hit the back of his head against the wall in frustration.

"So, an angel told you," said Lucifer. "Thank you for your cooperation."

He turned away from the pair and walked over to Mara's side. They spoke in low voices so Shem and Ham couldn't eavesdrop on their conversation. Lucifer first glanced back in the brothers' direction and then faced Mara.

"Something feels off about this," he said.

"You think they're lying?" asked Mara.

Lucifer shook his head. "I doubt it. Their reactions feel genuine. But something just seems strange about the whole set-up."

"How so?" asked Mara.

"If an angel wanted me dead and knew I was powerless, why send those two? Especially when it was simple happenstance that they attacked while Belial was gone?"

"You're right, the Redeemers are no slouches—these two are the exception to the rule," said Mara. "So they would send the experts, they wouldn't go to just these two."

"There's also the question of what would Heaven gain by killing me," said Lucifer. "The Divine Choir enjoys having me as their boogeyman. Killing me would undermine that."

"Could be a rogue angel, not the first time one of them has gone insane," said Mara.

"True," said Lucifer. "But this feels different somehow."

"So what now?"

"Anael," said Lucifer. "She knows about my condition—in fact, she was the one who first realized it. And Belial went to her for help when I was injured, but she refused."

"You think she's responsible for this?"

"I doubt it. Anael believes I should face culpability for

my actions and that can't happen if I'm dead. And this kind of duplicity isn't her style," said Lucifer. "But it does seem like the kind of thing a lesser angel would attempt. The only question is who suddenly wants me dead? And why use Bill and Ted's idiot cousins? Anael might be able to answer those questions for me."

"You're not seriously thinking of going to her, are you?" asked Mara.

"Of course not."

Mara breathed a sigh of relief. "Good. For a second, I was worried."

"No, I'm going to summon her," said Lucifer. "That way, we can meet away from Uriel's prying ears and I can find out what she knows. See if she was aware of what he's been up to."

"I'm not so sure I like this plan, sire," said Mara. "I understand the relationship you two once had, but you've been through a lot with each other just in the past few months."

"I know, but I don't have a whole lot of options here, Mara," said Lucifer.

She sighed. "Fine, but you have to let me help you with it."

Lucifer nodded. "I was actually hoping you'd say that. Without my powers, my access to magic is a bit limited, too."

"One more thing, though." Mara jerked her thumb over her shoulder, pointing back at Shem and Ham. "What about those two?"

"Drop them off at the nearest police station," said Lucifer. "That van of theirs is no doubt registered in one of their names and should have been picked up by the cops by now. And as I recall, Chicago has very strict gun laws. So let the humans deal with them."

"And you're *sure* torture is out of the question?"

"Please, Mara, just do as I ask," said Lucifer. "And make it quick. It's probably best if we summon Anael from my home instead of this place."

Upon returning to the mansion, Lucifer began the preparations for the summoning ritual. He painted a sigil on the floor in the basement and lined it with candles. Mara stood in the corner of the room with her arms folded, watching him go about his work with a sense of apprehension.

She was no stranger to magic or summoning rituals, but the notion of summoning an angel left her feeling uneasy. There was no telling what would happen once Anael materialized in that circle. And though Lucifer assured her that Anael would be constrained within the boundaries, Mara still wasn't very comfortable.

Lucifer stood once he lit the final candle and did a final look at his work. He gave a nod and then glanced in Mara's direction. "All set. I'm ready for your part in this."

Mara was apprehensive as she moved from the wall and over to the edge of the circle. "Have I mentioned yet that I don't think this is such a good idea?"

"You offered to help," Lucifer gently reminded her.

"I know, but it doesn't mean I have to like the plan," said Mara. "Maybe we should at least call Belial. Or some of the demons from Lust. Having some back-up isn't a bad thing."

"I don't want Anael to view this as some sort of attack," said Lucifer. "Bad enough she'll be restrained within the circle. Having a squad of demons gathered around could make her uncooperative."

Mara sighed but ultimately acquiesced. "Okay, what should I do?"

"Get on your knees, facing the circle."

Mara moved to the circle's edge and carefully got down first on one knee and then brought the other one in. She sensed Lucifer moving behind her and then she felt his fingertips gently touching the sides of her head. Lucifer started chanting in Enochian and Mara closed her eyes.

Power started to flow from Mara's body into Lucifer's hands. He continued chanting the spell and the energy moved from the pair and into the sigil, which started to glow as it charged. The candles flickered and the intensity of the tiny flames grew.

Within the circle, the air distorted and bright, blue lights started to flash. Wind started to blow, moving rapidly inside the confines of the circle and the sigil faded as a figure took shape.

As the energy died down, the figure came into full view, kneeling in the center of the sigil, feathered wings wrapped around her form. She slowly rose to a standing position and looked at the two who stood before her. Anael tried to step forward, but found herself blocked by the invisible power of the mystic boundary.

"What's the meaning of this?" she asked. "This some sort of payback because I refused to help Belial after you were attacked?"

"No, it's got nothing to do with that," said Lucifer. "Although now that you mention it, thanks ever so much for your lack of assistance. Truly, I was touched by how little you cared."

"It's not my job to bail you out whenever you have to face the consequences for your own actions," said Anael.

"Never said it was. But a little aid when I was trying to do the right thing would have been nice."

"Ever consider that perhaps the right thing would be returning to the throne?"

"I hate to interrupt your lover's quarrel, but is this really the best use of our time?" asked Mara.

Anael turned her attention to the demon and narrowed her crystal-blue eyes at her. "And who is she?"

"Her name is Mara—" began Lucifer.

"Please don't use my name…" muttered Mara.

"And she's just here to help me, since my powers are still lost," said Lucifer.

"If not revenge, then why *am* I here?" asked Anael.

"Because I was attacked," said Lucifer.

"Is that really a cause for surprise?"

"Not exactly, but it is a cause for concern," said Lucifer. "Especially considering that only a few individuals are aware of my present condition. So the question is how did two incompetent demon-hunters not only know my address, but also that I couldn't defend myself?"

Anael shrugged. "How should I know?"

"Because you're the one who sent them," said Mara.

Anael glared at the demon. "That's quite an accusation. Would you be so confident making it if not for this barrier?"

"We questioned them, we know their information came from an angel," said Lucifer.

"And so naturally you believed them and are now prepared to string me up," said Anael.

"I don't see a flaw in this plan," said Mara.

"The flaw is that I had nothing to do with any attack on the Adversary," said Anael.

"Motive and opportunity," said Mara, holding up a finger to count both points.

"You'd also be wrong on both," said Anael. "I've made it quite clear that my goal is to see the Adversary return to Hell. What exactly do I gain by having him killed?"

"I have no idea, but I also don't understand Tom Cruise's scientology boner," said Mara. "Cultist behavior has always been a mystery to me."

"And yet you worship the Devil," said Anael.

Mara's eyes flashed with anger and hellfire began crackling around her fingers. Anael's azure eyes responded with a similar display of power.

"Go on," said the angel. "Let's see how tough you are when there's not a magic wall for you to hide behind."

"Ladies, please," said Lucifer. "Although it would be entertaining, there are unfortunately more pressing matters that take priority over a catfight."

"This is insanity," said Anael. "You know me. You know that despite our differences, I have no desire to see you dead."

"I don't think you're responsible, Anael," said Lucifer. "But I also don't think whoever it is intended for me to be killed. Otherwise, there would be no reason to send two of the dumbest, most incompetent hunters I've ever seen."

"If you're not blaming me for this, then why summon me? Why bind me like this?"

"The barrier was just to keep you in place so I'd have a chance to explain. I didn't want to run the risk that you'd fly off the handle."

"Fine, then how about taking off the locks?"

"Oh, you can't be serious…" said Mara.

"It's fine," said Lucifer. "If Ana says she's willing to play nice, then I'll take her at her word."

Lucifer knelt down beside the sigil and scraped off some of the paint with his fingernail. With the line broken, Anael was free to step out of the circle, her wings receding into her back as she did.

"That's better," she said. "Now, why summon me?"

"Even though I don't think you're behind this, you're the only angel who knew of my condition," said Lucifer.

"You never considered that these two might have been lying?" asked Anael.

"Even without my powers, I'm a fairly good judge of character. And these boys are too stupid to convincingly lie to me," said Lucifer. "Besides you and Belial, the only other people who knew were a pair of government agents, and they have no reason to go to these lengths. So my question for you is did you tell anyone else about my condition?"

Anael shook her head. "No."

Lucifer raised an eyebrow. "You're certain of that?"

"I think I would remember if I mentioned it in passing. You're not exactly a topic I like to spend much time discussing."

"Fair enough," said Lucifer. "But what about Uriel? He is your commanding officer, so to speak, isn't he?"

"Yes, but we have an arrangement. When it comes to the subject of the Adversary, he's allowed me full autonomy. I haven't told him anything about your condition."

"And why not?" asked Lucifer.

"Because it's frankly irrelevant," said Anael. "Whether you're powerless or not wouldn't change the Choir's position. They want you back in Hell, period."

Lucifer paused, dwelling on those words. *They want you back in Hell.* It was true, that's what the Choir wanted more than anything else. The Devil to use as an existential threat to keep the other angels in line. And Uriel's purpose was to see to it that Lucifer returned to Hell.

"Of course," said Lucifer. "Uriel sent them."

"What makes you say that?" asked Anael.

"Think about it," said Lucifer. "Uriel sends two hunters after me. His contacts could have easily found out that Belial is now working with Black on the side, perhaps even pay off Black's men to arrange for a job to take Belial out of the house at a certain time."

"And without protection, you'd be vulnerable," said Mara.

"Precisely. Uriel hired those two *because* he knew they would fail," said Lucifer.

"Why would he do that?" asked Anael. "What's the point of arranging a hit that's designed to fail?"

"Because of what I'd do next," said Lucifer. "I'd wager that Uriel believed I'd be so shaken up by the event, that I'd immediately return to Hell."

"Aren't you forgetting something?" asked Anael. "How would Uriel have known if I didn't tell him?"

"So you say," said Mara. "I maintain you're still the most-likely suspect. Wouldn't be the first time you betrayed the Morningstar."

"No, she's telling the truth," said Lucifer. "But Ana, answer me this—when Belial told you about my condition, were you in Eden?"

Anael nodded slowly. "Yes, but what does that mean? We were alone."

"So you thought," said Lucifer. "You think Uriel doesn't have secret surveillance in that place? Nothing is said that he isn't aware of."

"You're saying he spied on me?"

"Clearly," said Lucifer.

Anael's face was a mask of barely restrained rage. Her eyes flashed with blue light as her wings extended and enveloped her. Inside less than a blink, she was gone.

"That was rude," said Mara.

"It was also according to plan," said Lucifer.

"Huh?" Mara rubbed the back of her neck. "According to what plan?"

"According to mine. As soon as Shem mentioned the angel, I knew it had to be Uriel."

"Why didn't you say anything?" asked Mara.

"Because while Ana was here, I wanted your reactions to be genuine," said Lucifer.

"So what was that all about then?"

"Ana now feels betrayed by Uriel, which will drive a wedge between them and serve as a useful 'fuck you' to that prick," said Lucifer.

"So what will you do?" asked Mara.

"Exactly what Uriel wants," said Lucifer. "I'm going to Hell."

CHAPTER 8

I don't understand," said Mara. "All this time, you've ruled out returning as the last thing you would do. Your commitment to that idea even caused Belial to rush out. So why the sudden change of heart?"

Lucifer had his phone in hand. He was busy typing a message and quickly sent it out. Then he addressed Mara's question.

"Shem and Ham were just the beginning. In time, Uriel will grow bolder in his attempts to get me to return to the throne. And if I'm going to have to make this trip eventually, then I'd rather it be on my terms and not his," said Lucifer.

"Which means…?"

"Which means I have no intention of reclaiming the throne," said Lucifer. "Cross sits on it and he can keep it. The plan is to return to Hell, restore my powers, then resume the hunt for the Cocytus escapees."

"What happens once you've got them all?"

"Then it's time for Uriel to face some consequences for *his* actions," said Lucifer. "And at that point, I promise you that he'll regret attempting to play these little games with my life."

"Wouldn't that be taking a massive risk, going after an ambassador of the Choir?" asked Mara.

Lucifer smiled. "Not if he's fallen out of favor."

"And just how will that happen?"

"In due time," said Lucifer.

There was a burst of hellfire that started to take form right in the middle of the basement. Lucifer wasn't the least bit surprised, suggesting that he had expected this to happen. Within moments, the hellfire had become the form of a figure with demonic wings. They receded into the back and Belial stood before them.

"Ah good, you got my message," said Lucifer. "I was worried you would just ignore it."

"You're serious about this?" asked Belial. "You really mean to return to Hell and reclaim what's yours?"

"If by 'what's mine,' you mean my powers, then yes. But I don't want to hear any talk of the throne," said Lucifer.

"Understood. And in this matter, of course I shall accompany you."

"Actually, you won't," said Lucifer, then pointed at Mara. "*She* will."

"What?" The question was posed by Mara and Belial speaking in unison.

"Is this due to my recent behavior? If so, then I assure you, it was only because I felt it was the best course of action," said Belial.

Lucifer stepped up to his bodyguard and placed a hand on his shoulder. "I appreciate that, sincerely. But that's not the reason why. You've been working a lot with Odysseus and his men recently, and should you suddenly disappear without explanation, it might raise some questions as to what you're up to—or more specifically, what *I'm* up to. And I can't have that.

"But as Lilith's representative here on Earth, Mara has a lot more freedom. She can move about without questions being raised. And as such, she still has more connections with Hell that may be of use to me," Lucifer continued.

"I can understand your logic, but it feels like there's more involved," said Belial.

"Oh, there assuredly is," said Lucifer. "I want you to use your connections with Black, see if you can get into Eden."

"I need no invitation," said Belial.

"Not if you want to cause trouble, true," said Lucifer. "But I don't want you to do that. Instead, I want to know what transpires between Anael and Uriel."

Belial grumbled. "Why should it matter what those two discuss?"

"I'll explain later. But for now, I need you to just focus on that," said Lucifer.

Belial's expression revealed his feelings on the matter, but he ultimately nodded. "I understand. I'll keep my eyes and ears open and report back once you return."

"Thank you," said Lucifer before he turned to Mara. "With all that said, you're my ticket to the netherworld. So shall we begin?"

"There's something else to worry about," said Mara. "You're not going to Hell as a demon or even an angel— you're entering as a human. The experience can be pretty overwhelming."

Lucifer scoffed. "I think I can handle some travel sickness."

"There's also the matter of what exactly your plan is.

Do you know *how* you're going to restore your powers?" she asked.

"Erebus knew that it was your abdication which weakened Cocytus. Presumably he may also know how to restore your powers," said Belial.

"He's right, this all feels connected to that place. And so that's where we'll venture first," said Lucifer.

Mara took a breath and sighed. "It won't be easy. Even before you left, you didn't really travel much through Hell. To get to Cocytus, we may need to travel through some unfriendly territory. Maybe if we went to Cross first?"

Lucifer shook his head. "As far as I'm concerned, there's no reason for Cross to even know about any of this. I promised him his rule would be free of my interference and I don't want even the appearance that I might be going back on my word or attempting a return to the throne."

"That's understandable, but no matter where you go in Hell, people will know it's you. You're going to need some protection from a Hell Lord," said Mara. "It's not the same place it was under your rule."

"*Is* there even any Hell Lord you're certain you could trust?" asked Belial.

Lucifer stroked his chin while trying to think of someone who might be willing to work with him. His eyes met Mara's and he asked, "What about Lilith?"

Mara had to cover her mouth to stop herself from laughing at the suggestion. "Sorry, but I doubt Lilith would be willing to do anything for you."

"I helped her secure Asmodeus's former realm," said Lucifer.

"Yeah, but she's still sour on you imprisoning her in the first place in order to appease the angels," said Mara. "Trust me, she's not so willing to forgive and forget."

"That's fair, I suppose. Would be nice if she could let go of a grudge after all these centuries, though," said Lucifer. "Very well, then I suppose the best choice is Beelzebub."

"You're certain of that?" asked Belial. "Outside of Leviathan, Beelzebub has experienced perhaps the most change of all the Hell Lords since The Fall."

"Yes, but he's always proven his loyalty. I believe he can be trusted," said Lucifer.

"Then I can transport you outside the gates of his realm. Once he's willing to grant protection, we can move on to Cocytus and speak with Erebus," said Mara.

"Good, then let's begin."

Mara clasped her hands together and closed her eyes, beginning to chant in Dimoori Sheol, the language of the damned. She pulled her hands apart, and a stream of hellfire linked them together. Mara waved her hands in deliberate patterns in the air, the flames trailing after. The hellfire encircled her and then reached out, flowing around Lucifer as well. As it moved around them, the intensity grew until Belial could no longer see either of them. Once they were completely obscured, the flames began to dissipate, taking the pair with them.

Lucifer closed his eyes as he felt the transportation begin. He could feel the heat and a sense of dread formed in the pit of his stomach as he lost all concept of what was up and what was down. Although he felt as if he were still standing perfectly still, at the same time it seemed that his body was being tossed about a void.

LUCIFER DAMNED

The thing that hit him strongest was the smell. The scent of sulfur is what struck every human who entered Hell for the first time. It was overpowering to the point of being almost crippling.

Even though Lucifer had spent most of his existence in Hell, this was the first time he experienced it from a human perspective. He knew to expect some discomfort, as Mara had warned. But he never could have anticipated something *this* drastic.

When Lucifer opened his eyes, a red haze clouded everything. He fell to his knees and started coughing. The smell forced tears to his eyes and he could hardly take a moment to breathe. That unease in his stomach strengthened and before Lucifer could even process what was happening, he vomited, spilling the contents of his stomach out on the barren, rocky terrain.

"I warned you that it's not very pleasant," said Mara, kneeling beside him.

Lucifer wiped his mouth, but remained hunched over for a few more moments. He still felt as if he had another one in him, but mostly it was just dry heaves. With the sleeve of his jacket, Lucifer rubbed the tears from his eyes and carefully stood. The smell was still powerful and every time he breathed, it was as if the air was hot and ash-laden. But he found himself slowly beginning to adjust to it.

"I'll be fine," he said.

"Not if we stay out here much longer," said Mara. "Come on, we should move along and hurry to Beelzebub's realm."

"Where are we anyway?" Lucifer looked around. The landscape was completely barren. Dark clouds filled the crimson skies. The air was laden so thick with fog that it made it impossible to see very far into the distance.

"The Badlands," said Mara.

Lucifer groaned at that. The Badlands were the ungoverned territory that separated the seven realms of Hell. They were desolate and dangerous. When one came to Hell, they had to quickly find a realm in which to shelter. But the demons who couldn't find one had to reside in the Badlands, which were populated by all manner of hellbeasts that could tear a soul to ribbons. Demons who inhabited a realm only ventured into the Badlands when they needed to travel to another realm. Those who lived in this territory were either quickly destroyed…or became savage enough to survive.

"I'm sure you're aware that traveling through the Badlands without any sort of transport is a bit of a risky endeavor," said Lucifer.

"We didn't have much of a choice, did we?" asked Mara. "You didn't want to go to Cross and we couldn't go to Lilith. So there was no other territory I had permission to enter."

Lucifer huffed but knew she was right. "Okay, so how do we get to Beelzebub's realm?"

Mara pointed up ahead. But before Lucifer could start moving, she held him back with a hand on his shoulder.

"Aren't you forgetting something?" she asked. "You're the Morningstar, every demon in here knows your face and you want to keep a low profile. So walking around like that is dangerous."

Lucifer looked down at his suit. "So what do you suggest?"

Mara held her hands in front of her, cupped over each other. She closed her eyes and whispered in Dimoori Sheol.

Energy started to materialize and swirl in the empty space between her hands. She gestured forward and the energy flowed from her hands and wrapped around Lucifer from head to toe. His clothes started to change form. The fine, scarlet silk suit became drab, brown canvas. It scratched at Lucifer's skin and transformed from a suit into a heavy cloak with a hood pulled over his head and casting his entire face in deep shadow. Once it was complete, Lucifer looked disapprovingly at his new outfit.

"Not exactly what I had in mind," he said.

"Probably not, but at least this will draw less attention," said Mara. She summoned her magicks again, working the same spell on her own clothing and transforming into a similar cloak. "If we look the part of vagrants, maybe we can get through here unscathed.

"You really believe that?" asked Lucifer.

Mara shook her head. "Of course not. But it's worth a shot. At least this way, maybe we'll be unassuming enough so if trouble comes our way, we'll have the element of surprise."

"Hardly fills me with confidence," said Lucifer.

The pair began moving across the terrain. And as they started their journey, they heard the sounds out in the distance of beasts and savage demons howling. Lucifer already began regretting his decision to come here, but he had no other choice other than to press on.

CHAPTER 9

Time wasn't something easily tracked in Hell. Lucifer had no real idea how long they'd been walking, but it certainly felt like hours. His legs were numb with exhaustion and his breaths had grown heavy. They hadn't seen anything in the time they'd been on the move yet, which Lucifer could take as a positive sign. Running into something in the Badlands usually meant it was kill-or-be-killed time.

Mara seemed unfazed by the trip so far. She showed no signs of fatigue or exhaustion. She'd also remained relatively silent during the trek, preferring to focus on the path they took. Mostly, she tried to keep to the road. Although it meant they were more likely to possibly come across scavengers or bandits, they were less likely to run into any of the beasts that roamed out in the wild. And of those choices, the former were far preferable to the latter.

"I don't suppose there's much sense in asking how far we've got to go," said Lucifer.

"Unfortunately not," said Mara. "What does distance really matter in a place where time is difficult to measure? One mile or one hundred is kind of meaningless if you don't know how long they'll take to complete."

"You're not the one who has human limitations to worry about."

There was no sun to speak of, though the temperature was hot nonetheless. Lucifer paused beside a rock formation jutting out of the ground and leaned against it.

"And on that note, mind if we give my human parts a brief respite?"

Mara stopped and surveyed the land. "We seem okay for the time being. But we shouldn't stay here too long."

"Thought those words didn't mean much out here," said Lucifer with a smirk.

Mara gave a soft chuckle herself. "Good point."

"You know what I could really go for right about now?" said Lucifer.

"Some ice water?" asked Mara.

"That would be nice. But more than that, a car. With really powerful air conditioning," said Lucifer. "Maybe one of those on-demand entertainment systems, too."

"Don't think you're likely to find something like that out here," said Mara.

"I suppose that's why they call it Hell," added Lucifer. He stopped leaning against the rock and stood upright. "I think I'm ready to go on. At least for now."

Mara nodded and they continued walking. More silence passed between them. To Lucifer, everything looked the same. But Mara appeared to have a sense of where she was going. Lucifer couldn't quite understand how she was capable of navigating the Badlands, but somehow she managed.

Suddenly, she stopped. Mara held her palm out towards Lucifer in a signal for him to do so as well. Lucifer did, then tried to see if there was something worth stopping for, but saw nothing. Mara remained alert, like a cat waiting for her prey to move. Hellfire forged a spear in her hands.

A sound came from above. *Woomph, woomph, woomph.* The volume increased. And as it did, a shadow flew past them, but was gone almost as soon as they had seen it. Lucifer's sight tried to follow whatever it was, but proved fruitless.

"What was that?" he asked.

The sound came again, once more increasing in volume. The shadow came a second time. Mara jumped at Lucifer, pulling him with her out of harm's way just as the shadow crashed to the ground. The pair rolled for a bit before coming to a stop. They both looked up as the dust began to settle.

It was a quadruped easily as tall as they were and about three times as long. The body had a thick coat of black fur and strong claws that dug into the earth. But lining its arms were sharp quills that also ran along its spine. The head had a mane of wild hair and its face looked like a mixture between a man and a lion. Serpentine wings flared out to the sides and its tail was like that of a scorpion's, complete with a pointed stinger at the end. When the beast roared at them, three sets of razor-sharp teeth could clearly be seen.

"Manticore," said Mara. "Just *had* to be a hell-damned manticore, didn't it?"

The manticore lowered the front half of its body, arms curled as its tail rose in an arc and positioned right over its head. Its crimson eyes burned against the dark fur and it pounced.

Mara pulled Lucifer with her as she jumped free of the beast. "Stay back," she said. "I'll try to draw its attention."

"And what happens then?" asked Lucifer.

Mara had no response for a moment. Then she shrugged and said, "To be honest, I haven't thought that far ahead."

The manticore roared and brought its tail down. Mara rolled away just as the stinger struck the ground. It swung the tail at her again, and Mara slapped it away with her spear. But that only seemed to anger the beast further. It dipped its head as low as possible and some of the quills along its spine fired.

Mara used a combination of dodging and ducking to avoid the projectiles while deflecting others with the spear. In her grasp, the spear changed shape. The front tip became a large weight and the staff section slackened, transforming into a rope. Mara swung the meteor hammer and hurled the heavy end at the manticore.

After it struck a blow to the face, the manticore flew into a rage and flew right at her. Mara jumped towards the beast, her own wings emerging from her back. She used them to evade his claws and threw the meteor hammer again. It changed in mid-air as it reached its destination, now becoming a lasso that the manticore's head flew right through the center of.

Mara pulled the lasso tight and held on as the manticore took her for a ride. It flew up higher into the crimson sky, twirling as it did to try and shake her off. Mara wrapped the end of the lasso around her arm. She continued to wrap it, shortening the length until she reached the manticore's back. Mara planted both feet between its wings and gripped the lasso with both hands.

She yanked on it and it tightened around the manticore's throat. The sudden pull-back forced the manticore to reverse direction and plummet towards the ground. As they flew together, the manticore struck her from behind with its tail. Mara fell off its back, but still held tightly to the rope. She flapped around while the manticore continued to try to shake her off.

They crashed together and the force threw Mara forward. Her grip loosed and she hit the ground and flipped over a few times before landing on her stomach. She stayed that way for a moment, stunned from the fall. The manticore moved gingerly closer, its head close to the ground. Once within reach, the manticore gave a roar and leaned in to feast.

A rock struck its eye. The manticore jerked its head in the direction, angered and distracted. Lucifer stood there, tossing another rock in his hand. He smirked and chucked it. The rock hit the manticore right in the nose and it bellowed to communicate its rage. It started on a charge, but Lucifer just stood tall and waited.

The manticore pounced and at that moment, Lucifer dove forward. Once he hit the ground, he transitioned into a roll, then sprung to his feet and began running. The manticore landed where Lucifer had stood and skidded to a stop. It turned and chased after him.

Lucifer chanced a look over his shoulder and saw the manticore building up speed, aided by the wings that propelled it forward with each leap. The beast raised up its tail and it lanced ahead, moving over Lucifer's head. He tried to stop and slipped, sliding on the rough terrain just as the stinger struck. It hit the ground right between Lucifer's spread-open legs.

The Morningstar rolled and stood, then ran again. The manticore continued chasing, firing off quills. Before they reached him, the quills struck a barrier of hellfire. Lucifer looked up and saw Mara flying overhead, the shield courtesy of her. She drew the hellfire back into her hands and reforged it into a bow. As she drew the string, a flaming arrow flared into existence. She released the string and then drew it back several times in rapid succession, generating and firing a new arrow with each movement.

The arrows cut through the air and drove the manticore into a frenzy trying to avoid them. Some it could evade or strike down with its tail, but others found their mark and the manticore yelped in pain with each hit.

Mara's wings propelled her down, continuing to fire arrows as she did. The bow changed shape again, returning to the spear. The manticore bent its back and looked up, then leapt to meet her.

But before the manticore could reach her, Mara hurled the spear forward with all her might. It flew right into the manticore's mouth and burned a path through its body, eventually coming out the other end. The manticore froze in mid-air, held for a moment, and then fell right back to the surface. When it struck the ground, it sent a small tremor through the area that nearly caused Lucifer to stumble.

Mara landed beside the manticore. With a wave of her hand, the spear returned to her body. She changed its shape again and now it became a flaming sword. Mara approached the manticore's head and raised the blade up, then plunged it into the beast's eye. The manticore remained still and all tension left its body, the tail and its wings falling limp.

"I thought the road was supposed to be safer," said Lucifer.

"Supposed to be, but the Badlands are an unpredictable place," said Mara.

Lucifer tilted his head and looked at the dead creature.

"It's a pity, really. If we could have managed to somehow tame it, this journey would go a lot easier."

"'If' being the operative word," noted Mara. "Manticores aren't exactly known for being easily domesticated."

"So I've been told," said Lucifer. "Anyway, shall we continue on?"

Mara nodded and they returned to the path.

Mara and Lucifer had been so distracted by the manticore that they never noticed the lavellan, a kind of large rodent, that watched the whole battle unfold. Once they returned to their path, the lavellan scurried off.

The lavellan arrived at its destination, where a cloaked demon waited. Once the lavellan came, the demon turned his attention to the beast. The demon knelt down before the creature and it stood on its hind legs. The lavellan began chittering away and the demon listened intently to the sounds.

"You don't say…" he said. "And you're certain it was her?"

The lavellan continued to chitter, moving its head and front legs to gesture. The demon nodded and then proceeded to ask more follow-up questions.

"With a human, you say?" The demon paused and waited for the response, then said, "No…not a human… but something else?"

Once the lavellan had communicated everything it knew, the demon reached a hand out and stroked its head. The creature closed its beady red eyes and chittered in satisfaction.

"Good boy, Joran is very pleased with your work," said the demon. "And I believe I know someone who will be very interested to learn of this information. Very interested indeed…"

Joran smiled to himself and rose to his feet. He was hunched over and had difficulty walking. His wings raised him off the ground and took him deeper into the Badlands, to a cave hidden in a cliff. There were other demons in here as well, all of them unable to find refuge in one of the realms. Joran moved past them, until he came to a chamber where one demon sat alone in a chair, manipulating hellfire between his fingers.

"Leader, Joran brings news," said the demon, kneeling before the chair.

The leader's hand stopped and the hellfire dissipated. "I'm listening."

"Lilith's regent, she in the Badlands. But she not alone."

"Is that so?" asked the demon. "And who has come with her?"

Joran shook his head. "Joran not know. But he no powers. Yet…no human. Something else. Something… different."

"Isn't that interesting…" said the demon. "Then, perhaps we should send out some feelers to learn more about our new arrival."

CHAPTER 10

Since the manticore attack, Lucifer and Mara had traveled over a wide distance. Although there were some slight variations—rock formations, a few mountains, forks and crossroads—by and large the terrain looked largely the same. The sky and the weather never changed and the horizon remained in a perpetual fog.

But change eventually did come when they saw the massive walls of a city pierce the haze. They walked along the length of the wall until they came to an entrance—a pair of massive doors with torches flanking either side. Two massive demons stood outside the gates. A tower just behind the wall had another demon, who drew a hellfire bow and kept the arrow nocked.

"Where do you think you're going?" asked one of the two guards. Both wore black, chitinous armor that made them look like demons wearing the hides of giant insects.

"We're here for an audience with the Lord of the Flies," said Mara.

"Only those with special dispensation may enter the realm of Beelzebub. We don't just let anyone come in here from the Badlands."

"I'm a representative of Lilith, which makes me an officer of the Infernal Court. And according to the laws of the Court, officers are allowed free passage between realms," said Mara.

One of the guards stepped forward and stared down at Mara. She looked right back up at him, not the least bit intimidated by his larger stature. He raised a hand and slapped it across her face. His strength was so great that Mara was knocked to the ground.

"Officers of the court may be allowed passage, but Beelzebub does not recognize the authority of Lilith," said the guard. "As far as he is concerned, Asmodeus is still the rightful ruler of that realm."

Mara looked up, her yellow eyes burning with rage. She waved her hand and the guard was thrown right back against the wall. The other guard raised his weapon—a large hammer—and charged at her. Mara's arm lashed forward, a hellfire bola flying from her hand and snaring the guard's ankles together. His momentum still pushed him forward and he fell face down.

The archer up in the tower started firing arrows. Mara raised up her arm, a hellfire shield forming to block them. Her wings popped out of her back and with a large flap, generated enough of an updraft to propel her towards the tower. She threw the shield and it transformed into a spear as it flew, impaling the archer and sending him falling back on the other side of the wall.

The doors opened and more guards poured forth, all of them armed with their own hellfire weapons. Mara landed on the ground and forged twin hellfire swords in her hands.

"Enough!" said Lucifer, moving between the combatants with his arms extended out to the sides. "We simply want an audience with Beelzebub."

"You attack our realm and expect us to give you an audience with our leader?"

"Your men threw the first punch, I was just defending myself," protested Mara.

"She's right, he *did* attack her first after refusing to obey the laws of the Court," said Lucifer.

"Regardless, we cannot permit you to pass through the gate," said the guard.

Lucifer took a breath and hesitated. It was his hope to maintain a low profile, so that no one would even know he had entered Hell other than a select few. But in order to get to Beelzebub, he'd need to do something. Lucifer pulled back the hood from his cloak to reveal his visage to the guards.

"Tell the Lord of the Flies that the Morningstar would like a word," he said.

The guards all wore dumbfounded expressions on their faces. Some remained battle-ready, though confused. Others relaxed their stances. And a few immediately expressed their servility by bowing before Lucifer.

"Apologies, my Lord," said the head guard. "Had we known it was you…"

"Yes, I'm certain things would have gone differently. Unfortunately, this wasn't the way I wanted to conduct business," said Lucifer. "Now, can we please be shown to Beelzebub?"

The head guard rose to his feet and bowed once more. "A thousand pardons, Sire. But Lord Beelzebub's decree remains in effect—he does not recognize Lilith's claim to lordship and as such, does not consider any of her representatives to be officers of the Court. This demon will have to remain outside or we shall treat her as an invader."

"This is ridiculous," said Mara.

"I'm inclined to agree with her," said Lucifer. "Mara is my aide and as such, where I go, she goes. You certainly can't expect me to enter what could be hostile territory on my own, do you?"

"But Lord Beelzebub…"

"You leave Beelzebub to me," said Lucifer. "I'll take full responsibility for your actions. But refusing to allow Mara passage would be like refusing to allow *me* passage. Does your master really want to make the Morningstar his enemy?"

The head guard hesitated. He looked to his compatriots for guidance, and they seemed to be at just as much of a loss. When he turned his attention back to Lucifer, he gave a nod of agreement.

"We shall honor the wishes of the Morningstar," he said. "Please, follow me."

The head guard turned and led Lucifer and Mara past the gates and into Beelzebub's realm. Each realm of Hell was governed in accordance with the Hell Lord who ruled it. This was far from the vision of freedom and independence that Lucifer had hoped for when he led the revolt against Heaven, but in those early days following The Fall, the only way to maintain some semblance of peace and prevent another war was to give his lieutenants rule over segments of Hell.

At the time, it was a means to an end. Only intended to be a temporary measure. But the struggles of those early days and dealing with the fallout from the Nephilim Wars and Abraxas's rebellion wore on Lucifer. He retreated further and further into his own empty realm and his lofty goals to establish a Heaven of his own fell to the wayside.

As Lucifer glanced around Beelzebub's realm, this failure was brought into stark reality. He had never actually visited any of the realms of Hell. But now he saw the rotting and dilapidated structures. There were people in chains out in the public square. Screams of torture filled the air and the stench of death and decay was thick. As befitting Beelzebub's title, insects freely moved about the realm, their incessant buzzing causing Lucifer's skin to crawl.

In the center of the realm was a large castle, made of the same chitinous material as the armor worn by the guards. Its architecture seemed almost organic and the walls looked as if they'd grown out of filth. The guard led them through the heavy doors and inside the large structure.

They ascended several flights of stairs, each step seemingly moving beneath them, as if the entire castle itself were alive. And finally, the guard brought them to a large dining room. A long table was stretched out in the middle of the room, lined with food. Guards surrounded the table, but only one being ate.

The creature that feasted on the buffet was like a giant insect. His wings buzzed as they carried his gluttonous form around the table and he gorged himself to his heart's content. His antennae twitched and his head jerked in their direction. The giant, yellow eyes hummed, laid out in the hexagonal patterns possessed by a fly.

Hell had a transformative effect on its denizens. The longer and more corrupted they were by Hell, the more extreme the transformation. Such was the case with Beelzebub. His gossamer wings flitted, carrying his large, stocky frame over to the other end of the table near the doors.

"Do my eyes deceive me or izzzat the Morningstar?"

"Beelzebub, it's been some time," said Lucifer.

"Yes, not since the last meeting of the Infernal Court." Beelzebub turned from Lucifer to Mara and his eyes carried a harsh burn of intensity. "Why is *she* here?"

"She's here because I asked her to accompany me," said Lucifer.

"I do not approve of her nor her mistress," said Beelzebub. "You remember my position on this matter, do you not?"

"Yes, I remember you speaking out of turn against me. And then I blasted you with enough hellfire to knock you unconscious," said Lucifer.

Mara's surprise at this comment was obvious by her expression—eyebrows arched to their fullest, wide eyes jerking in Lucifer's direction—but she said nothing. She would save that for later, along with questioning why Lucifer would claim Beelzebub had always been loyal to him.

Beelzebub gave a light chuckle. "Ahh yes, I remember quite well. But that was before you abdicated the throne. Left it to a half-breed of all people."

Lucifer walked along the table, examining the contents of the buffet. Most of the dishes consisted of insects and entrails, with nothing that looked or even smelled particularly edible, let alone appetizing.

"I'm not here to discuss Cross. Instead, I have another matter that we need to address," said Lucifer. "Cocytus."

"Oh? What of it?" asked Beelzebub.

"I need to get there."

"Why would you need to visit that prison? And why would you need to come to me?" asked Beelzebub. "You gave the throne to Cross, surely he owes you a favor and could grant passage through his realm."

"If I were to go to Cross, it'd be hard to keep my presence in Hell a secret," said Lucifer. "And that is precisely what I intend to do."

"Then the question remains as to why? Both in regards to Cocytus and the secrecy."

"My reasons are my own. You once trusted me without question. I see that's changed."

"You've made questionable decizzzions," said Beelzebub. "Granting Cross control over Azzzmodeus's realm, helping Cross imprison him, and then giving him your very throne. You can see why I'd be suspicious of your judgment, Lucifer."

"All fair points," said Lucifer. "And I wish I could tell you more."

Beelzebub stared intently at the Morningstar. His insect-like eyes hummed with a soft, yellow glow. "Ahh, I see now. You've lost your spark."

Lucifer looked away from the demon's gaze. He'd hoped perhaps he could avoid Beelzebub learning the truth about why he had come, but that was always a long shot.

"How could such a thing happen? How izzz it even possible?" asked Beelzebub.

"It's a long story," he said. "But as Cocytus was created with my power, seems likely I can find some answers there. All I'm asking for is some help getting there."

"You know, it's funny you should come here and tell me you need to get to Cocytus," said Beelzebub. "Becuzzz I've heard some rumblingzzz. Of increased activity in the Badlands."

"The Badlands have always been dangerous territory, that's not news," said Mara.

"Though I'd prefer your whore hold her tongue in my palace, she's not wrong," said Beelzebub. "However, this is different. I've even heard tell of demons leaving the comfort of the city walls to journey into the Badlands."

"That doesn't make sense," said Lucifer. "Why would they take on that risk without good cause?"

"My sentiments exactly," said Beelzebub. "And now, you want to go to Cocytus. I wonder if this has anything to do with the rumors of a new threat rising in the Badlands. There are even suspicions that perhaps this is not a newly arrived demon, but one who escaped the confines of Cocytus."

"Is that so?" asked Lucifer.

Beelzebub nodded. "Though that's not possible, izzz it? Becuzzz Cocytus is impenetrable. No one can break in, no one can break out. That is what you promised us all those eons ago, wazzz it not?"

"You want the truth, Beelzebub? Very well, here it is." Lucifer leaned against the table and paused for effect before continuing. "Yes, I've heard about these rumors. In fact, Mara was the one who brought them to my attention during her most-recent report to her mistress. As Cocytus was built by me, I felt it was my responsibility to check in on it. But I prefer to travel in secret, because if these are simply rumors, then I don't want to cause a panic."

"Hmmm…" muttered Beelzebub. "Would make sense, I suppozzze…"

"Now you know why I didn't want to go to Cross. If it proves to be nothing, then no one need know about any of this. But if it's something, then at least I'll have the element of surprise on my side. So what do you say? Are you willing to help me one more time?"

Beelzebub's gossamer wings beat furiously and he returned to the head of the table. He steepled his long, thin arms together and focused his gaze on the Morningstar.

"Very well, Lucifer. Tell me what it izzz you require."

CHAPTER 11

Beelzebub's aid consisted of a vehicle they could use and a small assortment of guards following behind for added protection. The vehicle itself was a carriage drawn by a basilisk—a ten-foot-tall scaly, six-legged creature with a head resembling an iguana and one giant red eye.

Outside, it had the same chitinous appearance as pretty much everything else in Beelzebub's realm. But inside, it proved remarkably comfortable. There were padded benches at both the front and back of the cabin, and the cushions were soft enough to sleep on. One-way windows ran across the entire circumference of the roundish carriage, providing a 360-degree view of the terrain. There was a driver guiding the basilisk, seated on the roof of the carriage.

Lucifer looked through the windows at their escorts. Four demons, each of them clad in the same armor as the ones in the realm, mounted on giant flies. The Morningstar then focused his attention on the sword that rested in the corner in a sheath. Without the ability to manipulate hellfire, Beelzebub had also generously provided Lucifer with a weapon he could use to defend himself.

"You're quiet," he said to Mara, who sat across from him.

"There's something I don't understand," she said. "You told me Beelzebub was loyal."

Lucifer nodded. "The little disagreement he referred to."

"You said he spoke out against you and then you knocked him unconscious," said Mara. "That sounds like a tad more than a little disagreement."

"To those unfamiliar with our relationship, sure," said Lucifer. "Beelzebub can be trusted to be honest with me. He's not some servile demon who will do whatever I ask."

"When you need some assistance, is servile such a bad thing?" asked Mara.

"Perhaps not, but those other Hell Lords only showed that kind of submissiveness when I sat on the throne. Now that I'm no longer there, how can I trust that any of them would still do the same?"

"But you were confident enough that Beelzebub would."

He nodded. "I was. Beelzebub is a friend, has been dating back to even before The Fall. He challenges me, yes. But isn't that what a good friend is supposed to do?"

"I get what you're saying, but I'm not completely convinced," said Mara.

"You don't have to be convinced. You just have to trust me."

Mara left the matter at that and decided to change the subject. "Once we get to Cocytus, how do you think it will all go down with Erebus?"

"I'm not entirely sure. All of this is uncharted territory," said Lucifer. "I was actually hoping just entering Hell again would restore my powers, but no such luck."

"But you're sure that Erebus can help you?"

"No, I'm not," said Lucifer. "It's a gambit. I just hope this won't all prove a wasted effort."

Mara avoided his gaze, directing her eyesight towards the window. Lucifer watched this and cocked his head slightly to the side.

"You *can* speak freely, you know," he said.

"I know, but there's nothing I have to say."

Lucifer knew she wasn't being truthful, but seemed better to let it lie for the time being. He too focused on the Badlands scenery—or lack thereof—as it passed by the carriage. Two guards flanked them on either side, and then one in front and one behind.

Something flew from the sky. It was a strange sensation, because to Lucifer, it was almost as if it moved in slow-motion. But he couldn't react fast enough to stop it. And though he could see it coming, it still proved to be a shock when the burst of hellfire struck the giant fly the guard was mounted upon.

The guard was thrown by the impact against the side of the carriage, his body hitting the glass with Lucifer reacting by sliding away. The carriage rocked from side to side and the basilisk bellowed in a mixture of fear and surprise, with the driver trying to control the beast by tightening the reins.

"We're being attacked," said Mara, looking out the window.

Lucifer craned his neck to try and find the source of the hellfire bomb. Dark spots hung in the crimson sky, but quickly they descended, growing larger. As they came into view, Lucifer had a sinking feeling. They were demons, but mounted on something far worse. Large, serpentine creatures with massive wingspans who freely spat hellfire from their long jaws.

"Dragons," he said.

"Can you see how many?" asked Mara, trying to look for herself.

"More than I'd like," he replied.

"Shit." Mara stood up and opened a hatch on the ceiling. She stuck her head out to speak to the driver. "Can you get us out of here?"

"What do you think I'm trying to do?" asked the driver.

Mara reached her hands up through the hatch and planted them on the carriage roof. She pushed her body through the opening and clambered out.

"What are you doing?" asked Lucifer, looking up through the hatch.

"Whatever I can." Hellfire forged a bow in her hands and she raised it up, then drew back the string to generate a flaming arrow. Mara let it fly, with several others in succession.

The dragons grew closer, their demon riders moving them to evade the arrows. They responded with roars that were followed with fireballs. Mara crouched, her wings flaring to life and cloaking her body to provide some protection.

"What are you waiting for?" she asked of the guard at the rear.

He looked up at the dragons hesitantly, then sighed and broke away from the carriage. The giant fly he rode carried him up to meet the attackers. One of the dragons dove straight for him and opened its mouth wide to let loose a jet-stream of hellfire. The guard's fly spun to the side, just barely evading. The dragon flew right by, but its rider leapt off the back, going for the guard.

The demon raised his arms and a flaming axe formed in them, which he brought down on the guard, slicing him clean in two from his shoulder diagonally to his waist. The demon's axe changed into a spear which he used to jam into the head of the fly. Its buzzing ceased and its wings gave up on fluttering. The demon jumped from the dead creature and his own wings carried him back to his steed.

"Dammit!" Mara cursed. She fired several more arrows, but all this seemed to do was anger the dragons and they descended. She gestured to the two remaining guards. "Go, go!"

They broke away from the carriage and flew to engage the dragons. There were five in total and the final guards were no match for their numbers. Two dragons apiece ganged up on each rider and made short work of them. Both ended up being engulfed by twin streams of hellfire and were left as nothing more than charred skeletons.

As their brothers took care of the guards, the other two dragons went for the carriage. One of them released a fireball. By the time Mara noticed it, it was too late to throw up a shield. The blast struck and she was thrown from the roof.

Mara's wings held her aloft and she used a hellfire whip to grab hold of the carriage and pull herself back to the roof. She crouched behind the driver's seat and said, "That was a close one, huh?"

No response came. Mara pulled herself up so she could look over the seat and see the driver. All that was left was a burnt husk. She sighed and opened the hatch.

"We've got a problem," she said.

"What kind of problem?" asked Lucifer.

"The driver. He's kind of…well…dead."

"Move out of the way," said Lucifer.

Mara slid from the hatch, unsure of what he had planned. Lucifer pulled himself up to the roof and climbed into the driver's seat. He pushed the demon's remains off the carriage and the dead body hit the ground.

"What are you doing?" she asked. "It's too dangerous for you to be up here!"

"You can't drive *and* fight off those attackers at the same time," said Lucifer. "So what other option do we have?"

Lucifer wrapped the reins around his arm and gripped them tight. His other hand clutched the sword so he could fight back if the situation warranted, though he wasn't as confident he'd be very successful.

Mara crouched behind Lucifer's seat, waiting for one of the dragons to get closer. She hurled her hellfire spear. The dragon ducked its head, and its rider was punished for that. The spear went right through his chest, dissipating as it emerged from his back, and he slipped off the dragon's back.

In the time it took for the rider to fall, Mara leapt from the carriage and her hellfire whip lashed around the dragon's neck. She pulled herself onto its back and used her hellfire whip to steer the beast away from Lucifer. In the process, her dragon slammed into one of the others. That caused the new dragon to reflexively spit out a jet-stream. Mara's dragon also took offense. She retracted her whip and let her wings carry her from the dragon's back. With the two having angered each other, they now ignored the carriage and instead started fighting amongst themselves.

Back at the carriage, Lucifer had two dragons to contend with. They flanked him on either side and he spied the two of them beginning to position their heads for a pincer attack. Lucifer pulled hard on the reins and the basilisk grunted and protested, then skidded to a stop.

The beast turned as it came to a sudden halt, but the carriage still had momentum behind it and swung ahead of the basilisk. Lucifer tightened his grip on the reins, but couldn't take his eyes off the two dragons that had flanked him. He stopped just before they initiated their attack and it was too late for them to stop now. Both dragons breathed fire right onto each other's face that had been meant for Lucifer and they both ended up killing each other in the process.

Lucifer rested his sword on his shoulder, admiring his handiwork. He would quickly realize that was a mistake once the remaining dragon swooped down. The rider snatched Lucifer with a thrown net of hellfire. Lucifer tried to extricate himself, but the rider pulled him from the carriage. He hung in the middle of the air, his body hitting the dragon's side.

"I've got him! I've got him!" shouted the rider. "The master will be pleased!"

"Mara!" Lucifer shouted. "A little help?"

Mara looked away from the dragons she'd managed to turn against each other. As soon as she realized Lucifer was being carted off, Mara's wings carried her after the kidnapper. The rider looked back and saw her flying after him. He hurled several hellfire projectiles with his free hand. Despite Mara's swift maneuvers, the rider blanketed the air with them and she was forced to deflect with hellfire weapons and shields of her own. As she defended herself, the rider used one final burst, pooling the hellfire in the palm of his hand. He threw it and when it struck Mara's shield, an explosion followed. Lucifer tried to see through the flames and smoke, but by the time they faded, there was no sign of Mara at all.

Lucifer quickly came to the conclusion that if he was going to get out of this, he would have to do it on his own. He still had the sword, though it wasn't a whole lot of use against cutting through hellfire. But if the rider's concentration was split enough, that might work.

"Who's this master you mentioned?" asked Lucifer.

"You'll find out soon enough."

"Ever consider what he might do to you once you've outlived your usefulness?" asked Lucifer. "Or what might happen when the other Hell Lords learn about what you've done?"

"Shut up!" shouted the rider. "You're not gonna scare me with any of your threats!"

"Not a threat, more of a promise," said Lucifer. "You *do* know who I am, don't you? And you know what kind of power and respect I still command down here?"

For a brief moment, the rider glanced to Lucifer. And in that moment, Lucifer saw the rider's growing uncertainty. It was working.

"Are you sure you want to make the Morningstar your enemy, kid?" he asked.

The rider bit his lower lip. And in that instance, his concentration faltered. The net weakened and Lucifer was able to reach a hand out and grab the rope. He pulled and the net dissipated around him. Lucifer continued to climb up the rope. The rider tried to shake him off, but he held tight.

Lucifer used all his strength to pull himself forward,

then released the rope. He jammed the sword into the dragon's side, using it as an anchor. The dragon protested by flailing, giving the rider some difficulty holding on. Lucifer pulled himself into another leap and this time landed on the rider's back.

The rider thrashed, trying to throw him off. Lucifer released the rider and tried to balance himself on the dragon's back. The rider turned and Lucifer jumped at him, slamming his shoulder into the rider's chest. The rider lost his footing and fell off the dragon.

Lucifer took the dragon's reins and tried to claim command over the beast. The dragon wasn't very accommodating and fought against him, spinning and flailing in the air. It was a battle just to remain steady on the dragon's back.

The dragon seemed to calm, but then suddenly flipped. Lucifer lost his grip and he fell, watching as the ground quickly came rushing up to meet him. He felt that the end was upon him but before he struck, there was a bright flash of light.

It was the last thing he remembered before he succumbed to darkness.

CHAPTER 12

Belial stuck a finger in his collar and tugged at it, trying to give his neck more space. He was dressed in a suit, something he never did, and he couldn't understand why anyone would wear these things. Particularly the tie. The suit combined with the sunglasses he wore was a uniform, though. Required if he was going to pose as Odysseus Black's bodyguard as the sorcerer visited Eden.

Although Odysseus rarely visited Eden, he had a standing invitation. All the powerful movers and shakers in the supernatural world were welcome through its doors. That enabled Heaven's ambassadors on Earth to maintain lines of communication in the event diplomacy proved necessary to resolve conflicts.

"You don't like the clothes, do you?"

Belial looked to the rear of the limo's cabin where Odysseus sat, his arms held straight out and hands resting atop his cane, which was planted right between his feet.

"Not in the least," said Belial. "Why do men wear these ties?"

Odysseus gave a shrug. "It's part of the formal attire."

"How does wearing a noose around one's neck indicate formality?" asked Belial. "Humans truly are a strange breed."

Odysseus gave a chuckle. "Just gotta put up with it for one night, m'man."

"I appreciate the assistance, by the way," said Belial. "I know you prefer to remain off Heaven's radar."

Odysseus nodded. "True. Eden's not my usual choice of watering hole. But you've been doing good work, and it's always nice to have the Devil owe me a favor."

The divider right beside Belial's head lowered and the driver glanced at him over his shoulder. "We're pulling up now."

Belial nodded and the divider closed. The limo came to a stop in front of the entrance to the Willis Tower. Belial got out of the limo first and held the door open for Odysseus. Once Belial closed the door, the car slowly rolled forward.

Odysseus led the way, Belial trailed a few steps behind him and acted the part of the bodyguard by turning his head in different directions. They entered the elevator and waited until it kept rising past the floors. Once they were alone in the elevator, Odysseus traced the sigil that served as a key to enter Eden above the buttons. The white button that allowed entrance shimmered into view and he pushed it.

Once they finally entered Eden, several curious patrons turned their attention on the pair. Not only was Odysseus Black a rare sight in here, but the last time Belial came, he nearly started a fight.

"What in the name of the Presence do you think you're doing here?"

The voice echoed throughout Eden, silencing the conversations and commanding everyone's attention. The guests parted like the Red Sea to give Belial an unobstructed view of the angel, Uriel. He stormed towards the new arrivals and pointed an accusatory finger directly at the demon.

"You're no longer welcome in Eden, you traitorous piece of shit!" screamed Uriel.

Belial's fingers curled into fists. If Uriel was prepared to fight, then he'd be more than happy to oblige. But Odysseus had other ideas and moved between the two.

"I don't believe we've been properly introduced yet," said the sorcerer with a beaming smile on his face. "Odysseus Black at your service, the finest sorcerer in the Midwest."

He stuck his open hand in front of Uriel and the angel looked stunned by the gesture. Odysseus took the initiative and grabbed Uriel's hand and gave it a good shake. Uriel pulled his hand back and regarded the sorcerer with a mixture of suspicion and confusion.

"You must be Uriel, our new ambassador," said Odysseus. "A fine sight better than the last one, if I may say so. Nasty little business that rogue angel got up to."

Uriel narrowed his eyes. "I've heard of you. In fact, as I recall, weren't you in league with him?"

Odysseus only let the accusation trip him up for the briefest of seconds before he came up with an excuse. "Well, 'in league with' is such a…strong choice of words. I was simply hired to do a job, but I wasn't aware of what he was truly up to. And he was so crafty, he slipped under the notice of Heaven. So I can hardly be found at fault for not exceeding the profound, celestial wisdom of the angels, now can I?"

"I don't care about you, Mr. Black. I care about the demon standing in my lobby," said Uriel.

"Ah, yes. Well, I'm not sure if you're aware of this, but Belial now works for me," said Odysseus. "He's my bodyguard, you see. And as such, he is permitted to remain in Eden so long as I am accompanying him. That *would* be in accordance with the rules of your fine establishment, would it not?"

Uriel's lips tightened and he gave a stiff nod. He glanced at Belial very briefly, but quickly returned his gaze to Odysseus. "Fine, but that also makes him *your* responsibility."

"Certainly, that goes without saying," said Odysseus. "Thank you very much for your understanding, my fine fellow. But we won't take up any more of your valuable time, so off we go to mingle." Odysseus turned away from Uriel and gestured for Belial to follow. "Come now, my bodyguard."

Belial gave Uriel a nod and followed. They found an empty table and sat down. A waiter came to take their drink orders and Odysseus requested a beer, but Belial simply held up a hand to indicate his refusal.

"You oughta have a drink. Might loosen you up a little," said Odysseus.

"I'm not here for drinks, I'm here to monitor," said Belial.

"Seems ol' Uriel there feels the same about you," said Odysseus. "Already I seen him whisper to at least three different angels. No doubt asking them to keep an eye on you."

"Let them watch me all they want."

The beer arrived in a tall glass and Odysseus raised it up. "Well, to the fine art of celestial spying then."

Odysseus drank and continued talking, though Belial scarcely paid attention. His attention was focused on the room. So far, he hadn't seen the reason why he'd come to Eden, and it was a good hour of just sitting and watching before she made her appearance. But once Belial saw Anael step off the elevator with determination in her eyes, his attention focused on her.

"There," he said.

Odysseus stopped whatever story he was in the middle of and followed Belial's line of sight. "So that's the little angel that Lucifer's so enamored of, eh?"

Belial ignored the comment and continued to watch as Anael finally located Uriel. She seemed insistent and soon, she walked towards the balcony with Uriel following behind.

"Stay here," said Belial as he stood from the table. He went to the bar and asked for a glass of water, then sipped it as he went closer to the balcony.

Anael and Uriel had gone outside and Belial pretended to watch the piano player as the angels continued to focus their attention on him. But he focused his hearing on what was happening out on the balcony. He filtered out all the other noise from the people around him and now was able to listen to what they were saying.

"I don't appreciate being given orders by those who are supposed to be under my command," said Uriel.

"Right now, I couldn't care less," said Anael. "I want to know why you sent a pair of bumbling assassins after the Adversary."

"I have no idea what you're talking about."

"Oh yes you do," said Anael. "You knew about the Morningstar's power loss."

"Lucifer's powerless? That's news to me."

"You're a terrible liar, Uriel. You and I both know you

107

must have somehow overheard it when Belial told me. And then you passed on information about him to a pair of hunters. Do the names Shem and Ham ring any bells?"

Uriel paused before continuing. "Where did you hear this?"

"Where do you think?"

"From Lucifer then. So why are you having little chats with him when you're supposed to be convincing him to return to Hell?"

"If you want him to return to Hell, then why in the name of the Presence would you send assassins after him?"

Uriel gave a chuckle.

"I don't think it's funny," said Anael.

"Actually, it is. If I really wanted Lucifer dead, don't you think I'd be able to send better assassins than a pair of morons who'd be lucky if their combined IQ exceeded their shoe size?"

"Then why do it at all?" asked Anael.

"Should be obvious, don't you think? To remind him of what he's lost," said Uriel. "Up until now, Lucifer has been living on Earth free of any worries, content in the knowledge that he's immortal and invulnerable. Now that he's been stripped of that protection, I wanted him to realize what's at stake. Lucifer cares only about power, so by sending those two after him, I've reminded him that he's now powerless."

"What are you talking about?" asked Anael. "If he cared about power, why would he abdicate the throne in the first place?"

"It's part of some scheme of his, no doubt. But I wanted to show him that his place is in Hell."

"Why not come to me with this plan of yours?" asked Anael.

Uriel scoffed. "Is that a joke? You'd never have gone for it and you know it. You've been reluctant to go as far as necessary when dealing with Lucifer."

"What did you expect me to do? Drag him back to Hell myself?"

"At this point, I'm willing to consider that option. At least you'd be doing *something* other than having social visits with him and his pet demon. Who, incidentally, is obviously listening in on this whole conversation."

At that, Belial turned away and walked back to the table. Odysseus had just gotten a fresh beer when Belial arrived.

"We have to go," said Belial.

"Why's that?" asked Odysseus as he stood.

"Belial!" Anael's scream echoed throughout Eden.

Odysseus sat back down. "I'll just wait here and finish my drink. Seems you've got other things to worry about."

Belial groaned and turned to face Anael.

"And what are you doing here?" she asked.

"I'm working with Mr. Black now. He came here for—"

"Don't. Bullshit. Me," she said. "I'm being jerked around lately by you, by Uriel, and by your boss."

"As I said, my boss is Mr. Black right here—"

Anael slapped Belial hard across the face, the blow shattering his sunglasses. Normally he would have struck back, but he decided to restrain himself.

"I've had enough," she said. "Where is Lucifer now?"

"Hell," said Belial.

Anael looked stunned. "He's gone back to take the throne?"

"For his powers," said Belial.

"Well, would you look at that?" asked Uriel, entering the conversation as he approached the pair. "After months of Anael failing to get anything done, I manage to do the job she was sent here for in about ten minutes."

"This doesn't concern you, angel," said Belial.

"If it happens under my roof, it's my business," said Uriel. "Now, I'd like to ask you both to leave."

Anael blinked. "Excuse me?"

"You heard me," said Uriel. "Now that you've failed your mission, I have no further use for you. It seems clear that your relationship with Lucifer was unnecessary. And you—" he looked at Belial, "I don't care who you say your boss is, you're really here on Lucifer's behalf. And you have no business in this place, period."

Uriel turned his back on the pair and started walking away. "You both have ten minutes to leave. If you fail, then you will be forced to leave. It's up to you how much of a mess you want to make."

Belial looked at Anael, whose face still bore the shock of Uriel's dismissal. "Anael, if it's any consolation—"

In an instant, Anael's expression changed to anger and she turned her incensed gaze on the demon. "Pass on a message to your boss for me, demon. Tell the Adversary that the both of you can fuck off."

She turned and entered the elevator and it was Belial's turn to be shocked. Odysseus came up beside him and patted the demon on the back.

"Well, that escalated quickly, eh?"

Belial sighed. "Let's just go."

CHAPTER 13

When Lucifer finally woke, he was bathed in darkness. He had to blink a few times just to confirm that his eyes were actually open. The place he found himself in was so dark, he even wondered if he still possessed his eyesight.

He moved his hands over his body and confirmed that he was still in one piece. There were no bruises or wounds he could detect by touch alone and he certainly didn't feel anything other than some mild discomfort in his back. Nor did it seem like he was physically restrained in any direct manner—no chains, ropes, or bindings of any kind. No sword, either. His only means of defense was gone.

The ground was rough, hard, and dry, with cracks and small holes in random places. Lucifer moved along the ground slowly, feeling ahead with his hands. He came to a wall and followed it up. The texture matched the floor. He could not reach a ceiling, and judging from the lack of a breeze, that led him to believe there was one, but it was too high to touch. He continued to explore the wall. It had a soft curve to it, not a sharp angle, so that suggested it was a natural formation. But he couldn't find any sort of opening. He wasn't even sure if he had completed a full rotation around the area.

A cave seemed the most obvious explanation for where he was. That didn't exactly narrow things down. It could have been a cave out in the Badlands or located within one of the demon realms. Now the question remained—should he be grateful or worried?

The last thing he remembered was trying to take control of the dragon. He fell off and before he hit the ground, there was a flash of light and then he woke up here. He didn't know how much time had passed. And how did he get here? Was Mara able to save and then teleport him? Was it one of their pursuers?

Another thought occurred to him, too—did his powers somehow come back? Could it be that simply returning to Hell *had* indeed restored him and all he needed was the right trigger?

Lucifer held out his hand and closed his eyes. He took a deep breath and tried to focus his energies on his open palm. In his mind, Lucifer visualized a spark forming and then slowly growing into a swirling sphere of light. The image in his mind was so vivid, it felt real. He was certain that once he opened his eyes, he would see a pulsating sphere illuminate the cave and show him the way out.

But when he did look, he still saw only darkness. He brought his hand right up to his face, wondering if it was a problem with his sight, yet he couldn't feel a thing. His powers were still gone, which meant the question of how he got here remained unanswered. And he was also left to wonder whether he was in the hands of friend or foe.

I won't just sit back and wait for whoever's behind this to show themselves, he thought. Lucifer found the wall again and felt around for a handhold. Seemed the only way left to explore was up. He reached above his head and found purchase. Lucifer tested the hold a few times before he pulled himself up. His foot found a small insert to latch onto and he could steady himself enough to bring up his free hand, seeking out another hold. Soon, he found that, too.

Lucifer repeated this process, climbing up through the darkness. Without knowing where he was going or without even a sense of how high he had already climbed, he had to be sure to do it slowly. Moving up too rapidly could result in him hitting his head or even losing his grip and falling back to the ground below. Without his powers, such a fall could result in serious injury or worse.

He kept his mind focused on the task, not allowing a second's worth of mental wandering. Once he escaped this predicament, he could concern himself with what had happened to Mara or why dragon-riding demons had attacked them in the Badlands.

There was no sense of time, so he didn't know how long it took him to reach the top. But finally, he reached a hand up and felt more than just a small hold for his fingers to grip. This time, it seemed like an actual ledge. Once he was satisfied he had a firm grip, he reached up with his other hand and found the ledge extended quite a ways up. Lucifer pulled himself up, and reached an arm forward. Solid, level ground, no wall. Enough room for him to climb onto.

Once he managed to get over the edge, Lucifer stayed on all fours and slowly inched forward, trying to find if there was a wall. But there wasn't. It seemed he was now closer to reaching an exit.

There was some sound out in the darkness. Light and

distant, but it was there. Or it could have just been his imagination. He decided to take a chance and continued towards the sound. Slowly, it grew a little bit louder and he knew he wasn't alone down here.

He reached a wall and climbed to his feet. With his fingertips running along its surface, Lucifer followed the wall. He shuffled his feet, worried about moving them too fast in case he came to another ledge without realizing.

In the darkness, he finally saw some brief flicker of light. Lucifer had to contain his excitement and force himself to move at the same slow pace. The light became brighter and he soon saw it was coming from just beyond a tunnel.

Once he reached the tunnel, he could now see that he was indeed in a cave of some kind. Lucifer moved through the tunnel, trying to contain his excitement of actually seeing something other than darkness.

The mouth of the cave was just ahead. Shadows appeared on the wall, created by the flickering light. Lucifer stepped through the mouth and saw a giant cavern with torches mounted on the walls. There were dozens of demons, stripped down to their waists with their wings proudly on display. They chanted and hollered in a joyous tone, screaming the name of the one they came to see.

All their backs were to him. Lucifer decided to use that to his advantage and he moved behind the crowd, trying to go around them. Or at the very least find some higher vantage point to see just what they were so excited about.

In front of the group, he could see a kind of stage— although it was really more of a small plateau. A figure climbed up to it and faced them, also dressed in a heavy cloak. When the hood was pulled back and the cloak dropped, Lucifer could see the man's face—short, dark hair with a chinstrap beard that perfectly framed his square jaw and mouth. It was a demon that Lucifer had never given much thought to, one who he'd imprisoned within Cocytus as part of a deal he'd made with Luther Cross.

Now, Lucifer could make out the name that the demons were chanting. And he remembered that Beelzebub had mentioned rumors about a new threat in the Badlands, one that had possibly escaped from the prison.

"Raum…" Lucifer whispered, though his tone was the opposite of the crowd's. Instead of jubilation, Lucifer spoke the name with a sense of dread.

CHAPTER 14

Not too long ago, Lucifer had made a deal with the man named Luther Cross. At the time, Cross ruled over a realm of Hell himself and his rule was being challenged by other demons, Raum among them. Lucifer promised to help rid Cross of his enemies and in exchange, Lucifer made Cross agree to do a favor for him later on down the line. That favor was what finally gave Lucifer the opportunity to abdicate the throne.

Raum fancied himself a liberator of sorts. An anarchist who wanted to overthrow the existing power structures of Hell. With all the Cocytus escapees, it never even occurred to Lucifer that some of them would remain in Hell, or that Raum would be among them.

"Welcome, brothers and sisters," said Raum, addressing the crowd. "I look around at this gathered assemblage of demons, and do you know what I see? I see the outcasts. Even in Hell, we're considered undesirable and we have no place. So since the time of The Fall, our kind has been forced to fight for our own survival in the Badlands. Out here, we are beset upon by all manner of threats. Harsh conditions and vicious beasts prey on us. All while the

Infernal Court betrays the very principles they claimed to have fought for."

Cheers erupted in response to Raum's speech and he paused to bask in their embrace.

"They're no better than the angels they rebelled against," Raum continued. "They said they embraced freedom, but what did they do the second they arrived in Hell? They formed a ruling coalition and divided this land up into territories for them to reign over!"

The crowd responded with jeers and insults directed at the Infernal Court. Raum once more paused and waited for his opportunity to speak.

"And in those territories, can anyone question their rule?"

"NO!" the crowd responded.

"Are the residents inside free to live as they please?"

"NO!"

"No, of course not," said Raum. "They've betrayed their principles and become exactly what they hate. And who's to blame for this sad, sorry state of affairs? Can we really blame fallen angels for reverting to type? All angels know is subjugation. So of course, the angels that first landed here would be the same.

"My friends, we know who is *truly* responsible for the sad state of affairs. The one who first spoke of the ideals we now strive for. Who could have turned this desolate dimension into a utopia instead of allowing his lieutenants to twist it into a dystopia. Had he simply had the courage to act instead of bowing and scraping before the angels and hiding in his tower, we could live in paradise.

"But he was a coward. He remains a coward, having abandoned the throne so he could live among the humans."

Lucifer feared where this was heading and he knew he had to find a way out of here. If the crowd knew that he was here, after how much Raum was firing them up, the result would probably not be very pretty.

But it was already too late. It wasn't pure accident that he and Mara were attacked when they were and it wasn't chance that he woke in a cave below where Raum was rallying his followers. Now it was clear that Raum had been behind both those actions, because he looked right at Lucifer and smiled.

"And now, my friends, we have him here. The Morningstar himself, the great betrayer who threw us to the tender mercies of his fascist followers." Raum pointed in Lucifer's direction. "Let's give him a warm welcome."

The demons turned to face the direction Raum pointed. And they saw Lucifer standing at the rear of the crowd, his back to the wall. A dam had broken and they rushed at him like a flood, screaming epithets.

Lucifer tried to run, but he didn't even know where an exit could be found. The way he came just led back to the dark cave where he woke. He tried to follow along the wall to see if it led to another tunnel, but a hand grabbed the back of his cloak and pulled him into the crowd.

They piled on him, tearing at his clothes. Fists battered his face and body and claws rent his flesh. Lucifer attempted to fight back, trying to punch or kick his way through. But their numbers were so great that he wasn't sure he would have been able to fight back even if he did have his powers.

It wasn't long before Lucifer was thrown to the ground. He tried to crawl to freedom, but the demons continued their assault. They kicked and stomped on him. Pain shot through every one of his nerves. He didn't even know which way he was going, all sense of equilibrium was gone.

A voice called out, dwarfing the screams of the mob. The taunts and jeers relented, as did the violence. It was only a brief respite of relief, for the pain still lingered. Lucifer tried to raise his body up, only to fall back on his face. The ground was slick with his blood, dirt and debris clinging to his skin.

He was rolled onto his back. Lucifer's eyelids were heavy and he tried to force them open. His vision was blurry, but even when it came into focus, the image split into two only to merge and then split again. It was Raum looking down at him, grinning.

"Get him on his feet," he said.

Lucifer was picked up by his arms, held out at either side. He didn't have the strength in his legs to stand under his own power and just hung limply in the grip of the demons who propped him up. Raum stepped up to him and clasped his face with both hands.

"Welcome to the Badlands, Lucifer," said Raum. "Welcome to the world you've created."

Lucifer tried to speak, but his mouth just filled with blood. His lips parted and the blood dribbled down his chin. Raum stepped back and watched the blood drip onto the ground.

"Gotta say, it's a real treat to see you in this state. You don't know how long I've wanted to have you like this at my mercy," said Raum. "The Morningstar himself. Revered leader of the rebellion and champion of the oppressed."

Raum punched Lucifer in his abdomen. Lucifer groaned.

"Wonder why they never added hypocritical coward to your list of titles," said Raum. "You put me in an ice prison where I couldn't move, couldn't speak, could do nothing other than reflect on how much I hated you and your lies. Hiding in your tower as the Court continued to become just as tyrannical as the angels you rebelled against. Just like the Presence, you became an absent leader."

If the number of blows Lucifer had received during the mob beating were multiplied by a thousandfold, they wouldn't come close to landing as hard as that one accusation from Raum did. Lucifer rebelled because of the lie of the Presence. If there was no supreme power, then Lucifer believed they should live in freedom.

But Raum was right. Lucifer had become exactly what he fought against. He felt it'd be sufficient to leave the Hell Lords to run their territories as they saw fit. He never imagined they would turn into the very kind of tyrants they once stood against.

More than that, if he were being truly honest with himself, he would admit that he really didn't care. Lucifer was more concerned with his own self-pity than the responsibilities of leadership. He'd failed in his mission and perhaps Raum was right to call him out like this.

"So pathetic," said Raum. "The Lightbringer reduced to to such a sorry state. You won't even fight back, will you?"

Raum punched him a few more times in the torso and then threw a final one at his face. Lucifer was nearly convinced that his head would break off his neck. He turned his gaze back to Raum and spat. Blood flew from his mouth and splattered on Raum's face.

The demon wiped it clean and kicked Lucifer in the chest. The force was strong enough that the two demons who held Lucifer lost their grip and he fell back. Lucifer slumped to the ground, but he was slowly feeling some strength coming back to his extremities. He groaned as he propped himself up on his hands. Though he didn't know what exactly he'd do even if he could manage to stand.

"Raum," said one of his followers, placing his hand on Raum's shoulder just as he was about to move back towards Lucifer. Raum stopped and looked at the demon, who continued to speak. "What should we do with him?"

Raum looked at Lucifer's battered and bloody body, struggling to stand. Lucifer got to his feet, but stumbled back and hit the wall. Instead of falling again, this time he'd managed to hold himself up, using the wall to help.

"We're going to do to him what he'd do to us," said Raum. "We're going to show the Morningstar exactly what it means to be trapped in Hell."

CHAPTER 15

Mara woke screaming. For her, only a moment had passed since she was caught in the middle of a massive explosion of hellfire. She could still feel the sensation of the flames searing her very soul. It took her a few moments to realize that she wasn't actually in the Badlands, but lying in a bed, wrapped in black, satiny sheets. She checked her body and found no signs of distress, but then she noticed that someone had dressed her in comfortable sleepwear. And the pain from the hellfire was now gone—what she thought she'd felt was just the memory.

She looked around the strange room and realized it was actually familiar. That's because it was *her* room—or at least, it used to be. Before she was dispatched to Earth by her mistress. Which meant there was only one possibility—she was back in Lilith's realm.

A knock came at the door and drew Mara's attention. She instinctively began channeling hellfire into the palm of her hand, but she relaxed when she remembered she was in a safe place. The door opened and a servant entered—a stocky demon who looked absurd dressed in a tuxedo.

"Oh good, you're awake," he said in a smooth, velvety

voice that demonstrated a sharp contrast to his appearance. "I am Kragmor, the mistress instructed me to see to your needs."

"The mistress," Mara repeated. "Where is she?"

"She's out for the moment, but will return soon."

"And where did she go?"

Kragmor let out an annoyed sigh. "If you *must* know, she is on business related to the Infernal Court."

"Do you know what kind of business that is?"

"No, she did not inform me of any specifics beyond that," said Kragmor and then added in a smarmy tone, "Perhaps because *her* business is none of mine."

Mara narrowed her eyes at the demon and felt the urge to channel her hellfire, but she suppressed it. He was just doing his job. Though she wondered what came over her in that moment. Mara had always just accepted statements from Lilith without question in the past. Yet now, she wanted to know more details.

"You're right, I'm sorry. I'm just still in some shock after what happened," she said. "I don't suppose you could fill in some blanks in my memory?"

"I thought you might ask that," said Kragmor. "Some of our scouts in the Badlands saw an explosion. When they went to investigate, they found a destroyed carriage, several dead demons and beasts, and then you. The only survivor of what appeared to be a battle with raiders. The scouts recognized you and brought you back here, where you were treated and then allowed to rest."

"How much time has passed?" asked Lilith.

Kragmor cocked his head to the side. "I'm sorry, what do you mean?"

Lilith mentally scolded herself. "Never mind," she said.

She still behaved as if she were on Earth and not back in Hell. "You said I was the only survivor?"

"Yes, that's correct," said Kragmor. "Though we do have some questions. We obviously identified some of the dead as raiders. But the others wore armor consistent with Lord Beelzebub's forces?"

Mara nodded. "That's right."

"May I ask what you were doing with them?"

"It's a long story," she said.

"I'd be very curious to hear the details of it."

Mara didn't want to divulge too much information. Even telling Lilith about all of this left her feeling a little nervous. The Hell Lord and Lucifer weren't on the best of terms to begin with. And if more people found out that the Morningstar was back in Hell, that could create further issues.

"What was that you said about things being none of your business?"

Kragmor huffed. "So, that's how it will be?"

"It's a very sensitive matter, Kragmor. No offense, but I don't know who the fuck you are. You say you work for Lilith, but for all I know, there could have been a coup or this could all just be made up to *look* like I'm back in my old quarters."

"Well, good to see Earth hasn't dulled your suspicious nature," said Kragmor. "Very well, I shan't press further. Though I have to inform you that the mistress will *certainly* seek answers from you."

"In that case, I'll talk to her when she returns," said Mara.

"As you wish," said Kragmor. "If there's nothing else you require…?"

"One more thing," said Mara. "You said you found the remains of Beelzebub's men and the raiders. Did you find anyone else?"

Kragmor pursed his lips and his eyes narrowed. "I do not believe so. Why do you ask?"

Mara just shrugged. "No reason."

"Was there someone else with you?"

"I'm still feeling a little fatigued from the whole ordeal and would like to get some more rest," said Mara, cutting short Kragmor's line of inquiry. "Could you tell me when Lilith is ready to see me?"

Kragmor bowed. "As you wish, my lady."

He excused himself and left Mara alone in her room. She climbed out of bed and went to the heavy, black curtains drawn over the windows and pulled them open. They revealed a balcony door, which she went through and then leaned on the edge of the railing.

It was indeed Lilith's realm, so Kragmor hadn't been lying about that. Mara had no way of knowing if Lilith had been informed yet that she was here, but she knew her mistress would have a lot of questions. And Mara wasn't yet sure what answers she should give.

Lilith eventually did return and requested for Mara to join her for dinner. With the aid of magic, it was a simple matter to weave together a suit for herself that was more appropriate for dinner than pajamas. Kragmor came to fetch Mara just before dinner and escorted her to the dining hall. The little demon hovered a few feet in front of Mara, kept aloft by his wings.

"I've never seen you here before," Mara said to the servant.

"I joined the mistress's staff shortly after you were dispatched to Earth," said Kragmor.

"I was here not too long ago to report to Lilith. Don't recall seeing you here during that time," said Mara.

"Perhaps I was simply attending to other duties at the time," said Kragmor.

Mara didn't know why she felt so nervous and suspicious. Especially since she was in the one place in all of Hell where she should have felt completely at ease. She didn't say another word and just followed Kragmor in silence.

They finally arrived at the dining hall. Kragmor hovered ahead and opened both doors, then moved to the side and gestured for her to enter. Mara stepped through the entrance and saw a table laid out with two place settings and a bottle of wine in the center of the table. Kragmor hovered over to the bottle and picked it up, then went to one of the place settings and retrieved a stem glass.

"Would you care for a drink?" he asked.

"Sure," said Mara.

Kragmor poured the red wine into the glass, returned the bottle to its proper setting, and then carried the drink over to Mara. She took the glass from him and sniffed the wine first before taking a tiny sip. Her suspicions rising again.

Mara heard the sound of a door and turned to the source. There was another entrance on the opposite side of the room from where her and Kragmor entered. And it was through these doors that Lilith appeared. Her red hair was expertly weaved and set on top of her head and she wore a tight black dress that clung to her curves. Her lips curled into a friendly smile when she saw Mara and her yellow eyes brightened.

"So, it *is* you," said Lilith as she approached Mara. "When they told me what had happened, I was more than a little surprised. Certainly wasn't expecting to see you back here again so soon."

"I wasn't expecting it, either," said Mara as she sipped her wine.

"Well come on and sit down, let's talk about it." Lilith then turned to Kragmor and said, "You can start bringing out the food."

Kragmor passed Lilith her own glass of wine, then bowed before his wings carried him off to carry out his orders. Lilith sat at her place at the table and Mara took her own seat.

"I was told that you were found in the Badlands. The sole survivor of a battle between raiders and Beelzebub's men," said Lilith. "How exactly did you find yourself in the midst of that?"

Mara sighed and set her glass on the table. She glanced at the door and waited for some sign of Kragmor or any other servants. Telling Lilith the truth was a necessity, but she didn't want anyone else to hear.

"Mara?" said Lilith. "I asked you a question."

The doors opened and Kragmor led a few servants in who carried metal trays of food. They set the dishes in front of both Lilith and Mara, then removed the covers to reveal steaming cuts of roasted dragon meat. Mara waited until the servants left and her and Lilith were alone again.

"I'll tell you everything," she said. "But it's a very sensitive matter. And I'm more than a little concerned about prying ears."

Lilith's head flinched back. "Are you saying you don't trust my people?"

"I trust *you*, my mistress," said Mara. "Everyone else is a question mark."

"Very well." Lilith picked up her knife and fork and started cutting into the dragon meat. "I'm listening."

"The reason I didn't come directly to your realm is because I'm not here to see you. I came here on a mission," said Mara. "And I didn't come alone."

"Who did you come with?"

Mara hesitated and looked around just to be certain they were truly alone. Then she said in a softer tone, "The Morningstar."

Lilith's knife stopped cutting through the meat. She set both her utensils down and reached for the wine, taking a long sip this time. "I thought Lucifer abdicated the throne for a life on Earth."

"He did, and it was his intention to stay there. Still is. But he's run into some complications."

"What *kind* of complications?"

Mara paused again before giving voice to this next revelation. "Lucifer's become mortal. No senses, no powers, nothing celestial exists in him any more."

"I see…" said Lilith. "But if he wanted to live on Earth, what should it matter if he's human or not?"

"For one thing, he still has enemies out there. In fact, it was just such an attack that prompted his decision to return."

"And he assumes returning to Hell can somehow restore his powers?" asked Lilith.

Mara nodded. "That's the theory."

"So why Beelzebub? Why not come to me or go directly to the new king?"

"Lucifer felt Beelzebub could be trusted and he thought going to Cross might risk being seen as trying to undermine his rule."

"And me?"

Mara took a sip and shifted in her chair. "You're…not exactly his biggest fan."

"That's a fair characterization," said Lilith. "So where is Lucifer then?"

Mara looked down. "I don't know."

"What?"

"Beelzebub provided us transportation and an escort to reach Cocytus, but we were attacked en route by raiders. Beelzebub's men were killed and I was knocked out by a hellfire blast."

"And the Morningstar?"

"Kragmor said no one else was found."

"So the Morningstar could have died in the raid?"

"Possibly, but I think there would have been some remains," said Mara. "Yet raiders aren't known for taking prisoners."

"No, they're not," said Lilith. "Which means this may not have been a simple raid. It may have been planned."

"Beelzebub mentioned something about a threat rising in the Badlands," said Mara.

"Yes, I've heard those rumors, too. In fact, that's why I was away when they brought you back. I was actually meeting with Cross about this very matter."

"But that means someone knew Lucifer was in Hell and that he was being transported by Beelzebub's people," said Mara.

"A potential traitor in Beelzebub's kingdom," said Lilith. "But why were you going to Cocytus in the first place?"

Mara sighed. "There's something you need to know about that…"

CHAPTER 16

Raum's followers had dragged Lucifer to a small chamber within the cavern. It was far smaller than the ones Lucifer had seen up until now and there was nothing really in the room other than some shackles hanging from the wall. They affixed the manacles around his wrists and ankles and then left him hanging limply, his body still weak from the beating he'd experienced and pain continuing to lance throughout his body.

Raum entered the room once they left and closed the entrance behind him. It was just the two of them now. He approached Lucifer and grabbed his chin, holding his head up so Lucifer was forced to look at the demon.

"It's sad, really. To see how the light has gone out of your eyes. To see how far you've fallen from the leader we all expected you to be," said Raum. "And now, what are you? A rebel who forgot his cause? A king who gave up his throne? A celestial who's weaker than a kitten? Such an absolute waste."

Lucifer began to chuckle.

"Something funny?" asked Raum with a tilt of his head.

"Ever hear of Gehenna?" asked Lucifer.

Raum nodded. "Heaven's prison. What about it?"

"Before the war began, the Divine Choir attempted to imprison me there. The tortures I experienced were unlike anything you've ever imagined. After all, where do you think the first demons learned the art of torture from? So if you think you can put me through any kind of suffering, just know this, boy—pain and I are old friends. There's nothing you can do that I haven't seen before."

Raum studied Lucifer's face for a few moments and then began to snicker himself. He patted Lucifer's cheek.

"Oh, my friend," said Raum before he gestured around the room. "Look at this place, what do you see?"

"Nothing," said Lucifer. "Nothing other than a pathetic demon with delusions of grandeur."

"That's right, you see nothing," said Raum. "No knives, no whips, no electrodes to be hooked up to genitals…none of that. No torture devices of any kind."

"I assume you'll be approaching something resembling a point soon?" asked Lucifer.

"I've never really been a fan of physical torture," said Raum. "At some point, the body eventually shuts down. The pain just becomes like white noise. You adapt to it, you become used to it. And what fun is there in torturing someone who can no longer react?"

Raum leaned against the wall beside Lucifer.

"No, I'm not interested in that sort of torture. What I prefer is to torture you with your own mind. Because it's true what they say—the greatest enemy we ever face is ourselves. So let's have a look at what's inside *your* head, shall we?"

"Do your worst, you little pissant," said Lucifer. "But just know that when I get my powers back, filleting your soul will be the first thing I do."

"I'm quaking."

Raum placed his hand on Lucifer's head, his fingers spread out over the Morningstar's scalp and digging into his hair. Lucifer felt the pressure on his head, like Raum's fingers were trying to burrow into his skull. But the sensation changed. It was as if white-hot needles were drilling into his brain. He opened his mouth in a silent scream and then his vision faded.

Everything turned white for Lucifer and slowly, his vision came back into focus. He was in a room constructed completely out of crystal, with an open balcony attached and perfect blue skies beyond that. As he looked around the room, his memory was triggered.

"Isn't this cozy?"

Lucifer spun and saw Raum standing behind him, leaning against the wall with his arms folded. Raum stood upright and looked around the room, nodding appreciatively.

"So, this is what the homes are like in Heaven. Very impressive," he said.

"What is this?" asked Lucifer.

"Isn't it obvious? This is your memory," said Raum. "We're *inside* your head right now, rooting around."

Lucifer heard a rustling sound coming from behind. When he faced the direction, he was surprised to see a large bed with white sheets. And a figure beneath those sheets, stirring awake. A man rose from the bed and stretched out his arms and yawned as large, feathered wings emerged from his back and reached their entire span. He moved past

Lucifer and Raum and stepped out onto the balcony, then leaned against the railing and looked out over the Elysium skyline.

"That's me," said Lucifer.

"Back in your more innocent days, I'd wager. But I'm curious why *this* specific day is the one that we're seeing."

Another sound came from the bed. Lucifer and Raum looked at it again and they both realized that there was still someone lying under the sheets. The memory of Lucifer came back into the room and looked at the dark-haired woman that awoke in his bed.

"Anael…" whispered Lucifer as he watched the memory of the angel with a soft smile on her lips. A smile he hadn't seen since that day.

Raum gave a wolf-whistle. "Normally I'm not one for angels. But I'd definitely make an exception for her."

Lucifer ignored Raum's comment and watched the memory of his interaction with Anael. He moved closer to them and reached a hand out. But his fingers just passed right through her.

"Sorry, no can do," said Raum. "Think of this like a fully immersive movie. You can look, but you can't touch."

Lucifer's fingers tightened into a fist and he rushed at Raum. He raised his arm and threw it forward. But all he succeeded in doing was going right through Raum.

Raum laughed. "You can't touch me, either. These are just projections of our consciousnesses."

"There's no point to this," said Lucifer. "This is all in the past."

"And yet, you seem to be pretty taken with your memory of Anael," said Raum.

Lucifer didn't want to give Raum any further gratification, even though it was clear that he was right. Perhaps Lucifer himself wasn't really aware of how much Anael had meant to him—how much he *still* longed for her.

"Every time Michael asks you for something, you jump. One would think the angel you never refuse would be the one you're sleeping with," said the memory of Anael.

"Ouch," said Raum. "In retrospect, that probably stings, doesn't it?"

Lucifer didn't respond to the goading, but he was feeling the same thing. He'd spent so much time trying to make Michael proud. And though Anael always understood, Lucifer now realized what a waste it was. If he could have that time back, he would have certainly made more memories with her.

The memory continued and Lucifer watched as he left Anael behind. And once he did, she started to fade, as did the entire room until he and Raum were floating in a void.

"Guess that's the end of that memory," said Raum.

"This is a waste of time, Raum. I know all too well what happened between Anael and myself, and I know the mistakes I've made."

"Do you? Well, let's test that theory."

The void quickly filled with a blinding light, which vanished as quickly as it appeared. Once it faded, Lucifer and Raum stood in a vast expanse filled with clouds, tinted with a calming light. There was a gathering just ahead of them, with the young Lucifer and Michael bowing on their knees. Surrounding the pair were celestial beings dressed in robes, each possessing six wings in total. Their eyes emitted light so powerful, it obscured the details of their faces.

"So this is the Divine Choir," said Raum. "The seraphim you once worshipped."

"I never worshipped the Choir, I worshipped what I had thought they represented," said Lucifer.

"And what exactly was that?" asked Raum.

A sinking feeling overtook the Morningstar. At first, he thought Raum's attempts to torture him with his own memories would just be a waste of time. He'd had eons to reflect on those memories during his time in solitude.

But a new sense of dread was rising to the surface. If Raum was going to scrape through Lucifer's memories leading up to The Fall, then he would uncover the reason why Lucifer chose to rebel in the first place. And that was something Lucifer had kept secret because he feared the ramifications of what might happen.

Those fears still existed in him today. Should someone like Raum learn the truth behind the great lie, it could lead to utterly disastrous consequences.

"Raum," said Lucifer. "You don't want to do this."

Raum just chuckled. "You're not talking your way out of this one, Lucifer."

"This is bigger than just you and me," said Lucifer. "If you continue to traipse through my memories, you will learn things that can't be unlearned."

Raum narrowed one eye while the other opened wide. "You're not making any sense right now."

"You have to just trust me on this."

Now the demon laughed. "Trust *you*? You locked me up in an *ice prison*! I couldn't move, couldn't breathe, couldn't sleep! The only thing I could do was reflect on how much I hated you and your absolute fucking hypocrisy. And now you ask me to *trust* you?"

Raum's anger became palpable, his eyes burning with righteous indignation. And Lucifer thought this might actually work out better than he hoped. If Raum wanted to unleash his anger, then he might forget all about his plan to torture Lucifer through memory. And then he wouldn't learn what really happened.

"Yes, I did imprison you," said Lucifer. "Because you were a threat to the tenuous balance that had been established in Hell. But more than that, you were a nuisance I had to get rid of so I could get what I want. I locked you up in Cocytus because it was convenient for me."

Raum's anger grew as he bared his teeth. Lucifer's memory flickered around them, like a television signal that was being interrupted. His plan was working, Raum was about to let his anger take hold and give up.

"You're nothing, Raum. Just an insignificant little speck who thought he could rise above his meager station. You weren't worth a second thought. Not then and certainly not now."

The anger began to fade from Raum's face, replaced with a pondering expression.

"Wait," he said. His muscles relaxed and his features reflected an understanding that had come over him. "I see it now. What you're trying to do."

"Now you're the one who's not making any sense," said Lucifer.

"Sure I am." Raum turned and gestured to the memory, which was now coming back into focus. "You're goading me into assaulting you. Because there's something in these memories you *don't* want me to see."

"You're insane," said Lucifer. "There's nothing in these memories that everyone in Hell doesn't already know. You've heard the stories of The Fall."

"The stories, yes. But there are at least three sides to

every story—your side, their side, and then there's what actually happened."

Raum gave a knowing snicker.

"Ever since I was sentenced to Hell, I'd always wondered just what it was that led you to rebel in the first place. How did you, the most beloved of all the angels, the golden child, turn into the ultimate rebel? What made some angelic scholar decide to ignite a war of revolution?

"It's a secret you've kept all this time, isn't it? And now here we are and you're still trying to keep it. You're still doing the Divine Choir's dirty work, aren't you?"

"I gave up any sympathy I had for the Divine Choir when I gave mankind free will."

"I don't think you did. Because for all your talk of free will and revolution, at the end of the day, you're still just an angel. A self-loathing one, maybe, but an angel nonetheless. That's why you never lost your wings like the rest of The Fallen. They rebelled in their hearts, but you never did."

Those words cut Lucifer to the bone. He had always prided himself on his independence and how he was willing to do what no other being in history had ever done—to stand against oppression and fight for freedom.

But it was all a lie. A lie that was about to truly stand bare and face the light for the first time. And all Lucifer could do was watch as it all fell apart in front of him.

CHAPTER 17

Mara wasn't sure what kind of reaction she had expected when she told Lilith about Cocytus, but she thought there would have at least been *some* reaction. However, when Mara told her mistress that Lucifer's abdication had also given the opportunity for many of Cocytus's prisoners to escape, Lilith said nothing. One would be forgiven for thinking Lilith hadn't even heard Mara's words. Not even her expression shifted. Instead, Lilith simply said it was time for them to visit the current King of Hell.

Despite the title, it was mostly just an honorific. The Hell Lords who ruled over each domain had pretty much no restrictions placed on how they conducted their affairs. So long as the Hell Lords stayed within their borders—as most were fine to do—the King of Hell was more or less a figurehead.

The carriage carried them across the Badlands from Lilith's domain to the center of Hell. Behind the walls of this land was a single tall tower where the King of Hell was the sole resident. It was the most sparsely populated of all the domains—less people were here than even in the Badlands.

The carriage pulled up to the front of the building and the driver opened the door for the passengers. Lilith disembarked first and just marched towards the entrance without waiting for Mara. The doors opened for them without aid and Lilith walked purposefully inside the tower and to the elevator. Mara caught up with her and once the elevator doors closed, they were alone once again.

"You haven't said anything since I told you," said Mara.

"There's nothing for me to say," said Lilith.

"Mistress—"

"You were on Earth as *my* representative," said Lilith. "Your job was to inform me of crucial developments. And yet you thought the walls of the prison housing the worst Hell has to offer cracking open wasn't notable."

"It's not that simple. The Morningstar said—"

Lilith pushed a button on the console and the elevator came to a sudden stop. She shoved Mara against the wall, her hands around the demon's throat. Lilith lifted Mara just off the floor, her yellow eyes burning with intensity.

"Correct me if I'm wrong, but it's *me* you work for, *not* the Morningstar, isn't that true?"

Mara put up some struggle, then nodded in agreement.

"That means your loyalty to me should trump whatever affection you have for him," said Lilith. "But instead, you chose to prioritize *his* desires over your responsibilities as my representative."

"I-I'm sorry…" said Mara.

Lilith released her servant and Mara collapsed on the floor, coughing. She turned back to the console and pushed the button to reactivate the elevator.

"Get off your ass," said Lilith. "We'll address your insubordination *after* we clean up Lucifer's mess."

Mara stood, still rubbing her sore neck. She stayed against the wall, as far from Lilith as the limited space of the elevator would allow. Mara could have never envisioned a situation in which her fealty towards Lucifer and her responsibility to Lilith would come into conflict. Even at the time when she kept quiet about all this, she felt it was the right thing to do.

The elevator reached its destination and the doors opened. The room was filled with a haze of smoke and the scent of burning tobacco was evident as they entered. They moved through the top floor of the tower, until they found the King of Hell himself sitting in a chair, paging through a large, leather-bound book. He closed it and set it down on the floor beside him, then reached for a glass of scotch on a side table, right next to an ashtray with a burning cigarette resting on its edge.

If Mara hadn't known who the king was, she would not have recognized him. Dense hair now covered the formally bald head and the goatee had grown into a full beard. He sipped the scotch as he watched the two of them with glowing, crimson eyes.

Luther Cross rose from his chair and moved towards the pair. Mara noted that he wasn't dressed as stylishly as he used to be. Instead, she was more than a little surprised to see that he wore plaid pajama pants and a simple black t-shirt. He then surprised Mara by throwing his arms around her and giving her a big bear hug.

Mara's eyes bulged in surprise. Her and Cross had come to an understanding of sorts when she worked with him on Earth, but they were by no means long-lost friends. His reaction was more than a little surprising for her.

"This is a nice surprise," he said, patting her on the

back and holding her tight as he swayed slightly from side to side.

"Y-yeah, it's…good to see you, too, Luther…"

Mara gave Lilith a look that begged for some assistance. Lilith let it ride out a little bit longer, no doubt because of her anger at her servant. After a few moments, Lilith finally placed a hand on Cross's shoulder.

"Luther, we're here for an important reason," she said.

Cross finally let Mara go free. He then gave Lilith a similar hug, but Lilith broke it fairly quickly.

"It's so good to see you both together again," he said. "Mara, you're lookin' great! How are things going up at Lust? How's Chicago? Y'know, I could really go for some Lou Malnati's right about now…"

"Luther, please. We really need to talk to you about something very important," said Lilith. "It's about the Morningstar."

Cross's eyes seemed to darken when he heard that title. "Lucifer…" He turned back to the chair and picked up his drink and cigarette. "Let's go in the next room and you can tell me all about it."

He started walking ahead of them. Mara and Lilith lingered in the room for another few moments.

"Lilith, what happened to him?" she asked.

"Being the King of Hell is a pretty solitary existence," said Lilith. "With nothing really to do and no one around, Cross…kind of fell into a bit of a depression."

"I thought he was going to make changes in Hell. Try to reform it," said Mara.

"He tried," said Lilith. "But the Infernal Court refused to work with him. Every time he tried to fix something down here, he was met with opposition. And finally, he just sort of…gave up. So now he just sits here in his tower and keeps to himself, no different than Lucifer once did."

Lilith left Mara and followed Cross into the next room. Mara waited another moment before she joined them. In the adjoining room were two loveseats and a large recliner, arranged in a U pattern around a glass coffee table. Cross sat in the recliner and both Mara and Lilith claimed a loveseat for themselves.

"So what's this about Lucifer?" asked Cross. "Hope he's enjoying his *retirement*."

He spoke that last word with no shortage of venom in his tone.

"The retirement hasn't been going as expected," said Mara.

"Good."

"Actually, not so good," said Mara. "When he left Hell, there was an unintended consequence. The walls of Cocytus became weakened without his presence and he's been trying to take care of the inmates that escaped to Earth."

Cross took a slow drag on his cigarette, his gaze fixed on Mara. "The breakout. Those prisoners that have been causing trouble in the Badlands. That's all because of Lucifer?"

"You've had problems with them down here, too?" asked Mara.

"More than you can imagine," said Cross. "Every time I hear from the Court, it's a complaint about the prisoners. I even tried to go to Cocytus one time to speak with Erebus, but he refused to grant me an audience."

"What's been happening?" asked Mara.

"Most of them are in the Badlands," said Lilith.

"At first I'd hoped it'd be a good way to get rid of

them," said Cross. "There's not much that survives long in the Badlands."

"But it didn't quite work out as expected," said Lilith, then she looked at Cross. "Beelzebub told her the rumors."

When Cross looked at Mara, his expression was one of hurt. "You went to *Beelzebub* before you came to me? After all this time?"

Mara sighed. "Lucifer felt it was more important to give you your space. He wanted to keep this under the radar, didn't want to be seen as potentially interfering with your rule."

"Can we focus, Luther?" asked Lilith. "We have more important things to concern ourselves with than you feeling snubbed."

Cross rubbed his face. "You're right, it's just…" He sighed. "I've been down here a very long time. This isn't exactly turning out the way I expected." He snuffed out his cigarette and then leaned forward. "So where is Lucifer now?"

"I don't know," said Mara. "We were traveling to Cocytus so Lucifer could meet with Erebus, but then our caravan was attacked by raiders. I was knocked out by an explosion and then I woke up in Lilith's realm. But as for the Morningstar…"

"His body wasn't among the dead," added Lilith. "We think they took him. And it seems likely that this rumored ringleader in the Badlands might be involved."

"And what's worse is he's lost his powers," said Mara.

"What do you think the raiders wanted with him?" asked Cross.

"If it's someone who escaped from Cocytus, then they would have reason to go after the Morningstar," said Mara.

"Maybe revenge or as some kind of a bargaining chip with the Court."

"So how'd they find out Lucifer was back in Hell when I didn't even know?" asked Cross.

"I think there might be a traitor in Beelzebub's court," said Lilith. "Would seem the first step is speaking with him. And you being the King of Hell means you have the authority to intervene in a matter like this."

Cross gave Lilith an uncertain gaze. "You know I'm not too keen on getting mixed up with others like that. And Beelzebub's hardly one of my biggest fans."

"Maybe not, but the Morningstar is missing and whoever is in Beelzebub's court may know something we don't," said Mara. "We have to try and for that, we need you to intervene."

"Yeah, I get that," said Cross. "I just want you to know that if I get involved, there's no guarantee we can keep a lid on this. The rest of the Court *will* find out about this. Not only would they learn that Lucifer is back, but it might also come out that he was indirectly responsible for what happened to Cocytus. You sure that's a risk you want to take?"

"No, I'm not," said Mara. "But the Morningstar is out there somewhere, possibly in grave danger. Do I really have any other choice in the matter?"

Cross nodded. "Guess it's about time I got out of this tower, huh?"

Lilith held out her hand and gestured to Cross's entire body. "You might want to consider cleaning yourself up a little bit. If you go into Beelzebub's court looking like a college graduate who moves back home and can't find a job, I doubt it will project the right image."

Cross looked down at his clothes and ran his fingers through his beard and hair. "I kind of like the new look. Think it conveys that I've got a relaxed personality."

"Right now, you need to convey strength," said Lilith.

A grunt was Cross's reply. He picked up the scotch and finished what was left in the glass, then set it down and stood. With his arms held out to the sides, he closed his eyes and concentrated. Ringlets of magical energy started to form around his hands and flowed inward, passing over his body. The clothes he wore started to shift, transforming into a three-piece power suit with a bold, red tie and a long, black trench coat. His hair receded back into his skull, until he was left with a smooth, clean dome. And the beard shrunk down, most of the hair retreating beneath his face, the end result leaving just a short, neat goatee.

Once Cross opened his eyes, he then reached inside his jacket pocket and drew a pair of sunglasses. He slid them onto the bridge of his nose and smiled.

"Okay, let's go save the motherfucking day."

CHAPTER 18

The scene changed again and now Lucifer watched the memory of himself standing before the Divine Choir once more. But this time, he hadn't knelt before the seraphim. Instead, he stood tall and defiant, even though he was wrapped in chains, seemingly tethered to nothing.

Raum circled the memory of Lucifer, admiring the then-angel's defiant stance. He gestured to the memory as he looked at the present Lucifer.

"You see? Now *this* is the Morningstar I idolized. This revolutionary who stood up to the greatest force of oppression in the universe and told them to fuck off," he said. "But I'm curious to see how this scene actually played out and if it's the same as the legends say."

The scene proceeded as it had in Lucifer's memory. They watched as the angels were dismissed, so only Lucifer and the seraphim that made up the Choir remained.

"Exile."

The memory of the Morningstar looked up, the ethereal chains heavy around his neck. His yellow eyes had burned bright, and he then asked them a simple question.

"If my crime was so heinous, then why exile?"

"Because, Morningstar, you still have a role to play. One that will continue to serve our cause for generations to come."

"'To serve our cause'?" asked Raum, looking at Lucifer. "What exactly did he mean by that?"

"To the Divine Choir, having a Devil proved to be a remarkable marketing tool," said Lucifer.

The floor dropped away, revealing clouds spiraling below, spinning off into a darkening void. Raum and the present Lucifer fell with the memory down the tunnel. The chains fell from the memory first, and the memory of Lucifer had screamed as he descended through the clouds. The darkness approached, and after what felt like forever, light appeared at the end of the tunnel. A harsh, bright light that seared the souls of all who fell.

Lucifer and Raum now found themselves standing in the desolation of Hell. They saw as the rest of The Fallen gathered around the memory of Lucifer. One by one, the blue light of their eyes was burned to a bright yellow by the powers of Hell and the feathers fell from their wings.

But Lucifer's wings remained the same. He went to the edge of a cliff and looked out over the horizon. The skies were a dark, ominous crimson. And when he looked down from the cliff, there stood the legions that had followed him into damnation.

Raum listened intently to the words of The Fallen—all of them expressing uncertainty and doubt for the first time in their lives. But then, the memory of Lucifer held up his hands and began to speak.

"I hear your despair. We've been cast out, separated from the light that had once nourished us. No more Elysium fields, where joy seems to dwell. Instead, hail this new infernal world

we now rule. And in this place, I see a new vision of our existence. Where you see horrors, I see opportunity. Because it's not the location, but the perspective. The mind can make a Heaven of Hell or a Hell of Heaven.

"So why should we care about Heaven? A beautiful prison with glass walls instead of bars is still a prison. Leave it to the angels and the 'Divine' Choir. Here, at least, we can be free. Here we are secure. They may have damned us to this hell, but I welcome their damnation and their hatred. And do you know why?"

There were shouts asking him to continue. And Lucifer smiled as he heard their chants. He raised a defiant fist high above his head, and then spoke a rallying cry that would define this new place for centuries to come.

"Because it's better to reign in Hell than serve in Heaven!"

The cheers echoed throughout the desolate landscape. Lucifer wore a broad, defiant smile on his face as he looked back to see his lieutenants similarly cheering him on.

The scene froze like that, with defiant fists raised to mock the Heaven that had rejected them. Raum watched with a broad smile on his own face.

"Impressive to see how they all once worshipped you so. But what happened next, Lucifer?" asked Raum. "What happened when it came time to actually rule?"

"Reality happened," said Lucifer.

Raum gestured and the scene changed. Now it was in a large room with a long table. There were eight chairs on either side and one at the head of the table. The former angels were in the seats. Raum walked around the table, making note of all the demons.

"Beelzebub and Leviathan, transformed the most by Hell's touch," he said. "Abaddon, Mammon, Vassago,

Nergal. The ones rewarded for their role, though they've largely been insignificant. And then there's Asmodeus and Abraxas. The ones you betrayed."

"I did no such thing!" Lucifer protested. "Asmodeus and Abraxas made their choices and they had to deal with the consequences."

"Of course," said Raum before turning his attention back to the scene.

The Hell Lords were animated, all standing out of their chairs and shouting past each other. Their screams and insults blurred together in a deafening cacophony. And as they shouted, the memory of Lucifer sat at the head of the table. His elbows were propped on the armrests, his fingers steepled together. The Morningstar's eyes were shut and his face bore a look of exhaustion.

"This is what the reality of ruling Hell is, Raum," said Lucifer. "Presiding over an unruly group of egomaniacs who all think they should be in charge. Arguments like this would happen every single time the Infernal Court held session. Border disputes, accusations of fomenting dissent, petty feuds, you name it."

Lucifer walked closer to the memory of himself. He looked at his own face and his expression reminded him of the dejected melancholy he had felt in those days.

"This was when it happened," said Lucifer.

"When what happened?" asked Raum.

"Lilith had been imprisoned in Cocytus, we allied with Heaven to overthrow the Nephilim and I signed the armistice which proved unpopular, and which in turn led to more sessions just like this." Lucifer turned and looked at his tormentor. "This was when I truly gave up all pretense that I was ruling anything. After this day, I essentially quit and resigned myself to my tower."

The landscape changed again and now they stood inside that very same tower. The Morningstar's memory was on the top floor, staring out over the landscape. Raum and Lucifer watched as someone entered the room. Seeing an angel in Hell was a strange sight, but there was Gabriel himself, casually strolling up to his brother.

"Lucifer," he said. *"How are you, brother?"*

"What is an angel doing in Hell?" asked Raum. "Is this what the Choir talked about? Have you been serving them the whole time?"

"Don't be an idiot," said Lucifer. "Gabriel had tried to be a mediator between Heaven and myself. He could understand my rebellion, even if he didn't agree with it. And the Choir felt it was useful for him to act as a liaison."

"Thank you for coming," said Lucifer's memory to Gabriel. *"Before I tell you why I've called you here, I want to start by saying that I'm not accusing Heaven of anything."*

Gabriel sighed. *"That's not a good start."*

"Asmodeus is missing," said Lucifer.

"What?" There seemed to be genuine concern in the angel's voice. *"Since when?"*

"I'm not certain, all we know is that he was last seen on Earth. And I just wanted to be sure—"

"Heaven had nothing to do with it," said Gabriel. *"The Choir knows what a violation of the armistice capturing or killing a Hell Lord would be. In fact, we're currently missing one of our own, too."*

Lucifer's eyebrow raised. *"Who?"*

"Raziel," said Gabriel.

"Do you think it's related?" asked Lucifer.

Gabriel shrugged. *"Possibly. But there's a more immediate*

concern. If Asmodeus is gone…"

Lucifer sighed. *"Lilith, I know."*

"She's your responsibility, brother," said Gabriel. *"You know the agreement we came to."*

"Agreement?" asked Raum.

"When she was human, Lilith had an affair with Asmodeus. She gave birth to the first cambions, some of whom evolved into the first monsters. The angels killed her and her soul ended up in Hell, becoming the first human who was transformed into a demon," said Lucifer. "After we cleared the field of the Nephilim, one of the terms of the armistice was confining Lilith to Hell. They felt she was too great a threat."

"So you betrayed one of your own in order to maintain positive relations with the very enemies you rebelled against?" Raum shook his head in disbelief. "You are an unbelievable hypocrite."

"I did what at the time I felt had to be done. Politics is about compromise. Sometimes it makes for strange bedfellows," said Lucifer. "It's easy to be critical when you have none of the responsibility."

The memory continued and Lucifer had said to Gabriel, *"I'll see to it Lilith is contained. You have my word."*

"Thank you," said Gabriel. *"And if I learn anything about Asmodeus, I'll bring it directly to you."*

Lucifer's memory gave a nod of understanding. Some silence passed before he then said, *"How is she?"*

Gabriel looked down at his feet. *"Why do you want to know?"*

*"You **know** why."*

"Lucifer…"

"Please."

"No, she hasn't said anything about you. Anael has maintained her vow to never speak your name," said Gabriel.

"You're still obsessed with the angel you left behind," said Raum. "One of your loyal soldiers was missing. Heaven was demanding you keep a demon in check. And in face of that, your biggest concern was whether or not your ex still talked about you."

Lucifer turned angrily towards Raum. "You have no idea what you're saying!"

"Anael betrayed you and you still care more about her than your own people," said Raum. "Even now, you're associating with her after leaving Hell in the hands of a half-breed."

"I failed, okay?" said Lucifer. "I know I failed as leader. That's why I felt Hell could use a different perspective on the throne, and so I gave it to Cross. You may call him a half-breed, but he's the son of Abraxas. He has the blood of The Fallen in his veins. What are you, Raum? Just a damned soul that used to be human."

"I see that streak of heavenly elitism is alive and well in you, Morningstar," said Raum. "I know now what an idiot I was to believe someone like you could ever stand up for the rest of us. Even in Heaven, you were considered to be one of the privileged. So what exactly was it that made you decide to rebel?"

Lucifer turned away from Raum. "You know what. I saw the spark of free will in humanity and I wanted the same thing for us."

"No...you're lying," said Raum. "I can see it now. You're trying to hide it from me, aren't you?"

"You're in my mind, Raum. I can't hide anything from you."

"Liar!" Raum jumped on Lucifer and somehow, was able to make contact when Lucifer couldn't do the same earlier. Raum's hands were around Lucifer's neck, squeezing it tightly. "Enough with these digressions, Morningstar! Show me what you're trying to hide! Show me why you rebelled!"

Lucifer had a sensation that felt like hot spikes being driven into his head. He had managed to keep Raum away from the truth, but now he had reached his limit. Raum was about to learn the truth and once he did, there was no telling what he would do with that information.

His defenses were at their limit. The scene of the tower and his memory of speaking with Gabriel melted away. And it was quickly replaced with another memory. The banks of the Styx, with a ferry arriving on the plane of Earth. Lucifer watched the memory of Michael flying off the boat, and just as his memory was also about to fly, Charon's voice kept him back.

"You're different from your brother. From the other angels," Charon had said.

"This is it, isn't it?" asked Raum.

Lucifer watched the memory play out. Charon had passed the young Lucifer a special coin with a unique inscription.

"If you would like to know more, then go to the Styx and throw that coin into it. I will come for you and take you where you wish to go. But a warning—do not let anyone else know of this conversation. And do not let anyone see that coin or be present when you summon me."

"This is where it started," Lucifer told Raum.

The walls were cracking.

CHAPTER 19

Raum stood before a massive, brick wall. He reached a hand out and ran his fingers over the surface. The wall had just sprung out of nowhere once the memory of Lucifer's encounter with Charon had faded. The demon craned his neck to look over his shoulder.

"You think this will stop me?" he asked Lucifer.

"I have no idea what you mean," said Lucifer.

"You're trying to keep me out. It won't work."

Lucifer just shrugged. "I can't be held responsible for what my subconscious chooses to do. Perhaps these are memories even *I* don't want to revisit."

Raum smirked. "All the more reason to see what's behind this wall. Don't you think it's time you confronted your own demons, Morningstar?"

He turned his attention back to the wall and placed both hands on its surface. Raum leaned forward, pushing against the structure. Hellfire started to crackle around his strained fingers, channeling into the wall. Cracks began to appear across the surface, oscillating out in jagged patterns from their starting point. The cracks crossed and joined with each other, quickly forming a web-like tapestry across the wall.

Raum's eyes burned bright and hellfire began to appear within the cracks. It created small beams of light that flowed back.

Lucifer knew he had to try something. He ran. Whether it worked or not was something he couldn't predict, but he wasn't going to give up to Raum without a fight.

We're in my mind, which means I can take back control from him, he thought.

Lucifer focused on what he desired and as he did, wings erupted from his back. They raised him off the ground and propelled him forward. He dove into Raum, his feet slamming against the demon's back.

Raum was flattened against the wall, his concentration broken and the energy fading. He spun and released a hellfire charge.

The blast succeeded in putting some distance between the two. Raum looked taken aback by the strike, but even more so by the sight of Lucifer's wings.

"How are you doing this?" he asked. "I'm the one who controls things here."

"No, you're not. I'm the one who controls my consciousness, Raum. And any decisions about what I can or can't keep secret remain my own, as do my reasons," said Lucifer. "I don't owe you a damn thing."

"We'll see about that."

Raum held out his hand and hellfire seared down his arm, forming into a sword in his palm. He didn't even wait for Lucifer to forge a weapon of his own, simply moved in for an offensive attack.

Lucifer ducked the first swing and jumped back to avoid the second. He couldn't concentrate enough to generate a weapon of his own. Even though in the mental landscape, he should have no trouble doing such a thing, he quickly found it too difficult to devote the necessary concentration.

"Don't you see how pathetic you are?" asked Raum between sword thrusts. "You can't even defend yourself against a lowly demon!"

Lucifer flapped his wings forward, hurling wind strong enough to keep Raum off-balance. His wings then lifted him off the ground and he landed behind Raum to deliver a kick to his spine.

Raum stumbled, but recovered and attacked with an upward swing of his blade. Lucifer pulled back and his wings instinctively closed around his body for protection.

The hellfire blade cut through the wings, sending feathers flying. Light emerged along the edging of each remaining feather and Lucifer felt the wings starting to fade.

"No..." he whispered as the wings grew transparent. Within moments, they had vanished.

Raum stood over him, resting the sword on his shoulder. "Well, well, how about that? So much for your much-vaunted control, eh?"

Raum swung his sword again, the hellfire cutting through Lucifer's body. He felt the heat searing his soul and collapsed to the ground as the pain radiated throughout every inch of his form. While he was on his knees, Raum kicked him into the teeth, a blow that threw him onto his back.

"Now, where were we?" asked Raum as he turned his attention back to the wall. He swung the sword in his hand as he approached, and once he reached the structure, drove the sword into the brick.

The sword flickered as the hellfire energy that made it up flowed into the wall. The cracks lit up as they had before, but now Lucifer could do nothing to stop it. He just watched as the energy flowed into the wall and more cracks formed. Soon, there seemed to be more breaks than brick.

The wall exploded, light flooding the void where they stood. Lucifer struggled to get to his feet and called out to his tormentor.

"Raum, don't do this," he pleaded. "The secrets you're about to discover…you don't know what they could lead to."

"I'm not a child, Morningstar. I want the truth and I'll get it by any means necessary," said Raum. "Just what is it you're trying to keep hidden?"

Raum stepped into the blinding light and when he came through the other end, he stood now in a massive library. Lucifer appeared by his side, which surprised the Morningstar more than anything else. Lucifer was able to stand again, but he still felt lingering pain from Raum's attack.

"Don't look so shocked," said Raum. "I want you to witness the moment when I learn what you've been hiding from all of us."

Lucifer remembered this library well. Located deep within Purgatory, this was what Charon had led him to. He saw his young self exploring the library, examining the unlabeled books on the shelves.

Raum followed the young Lucifer as he moved deeper into the library to investigate a soft, scratching noise off in the distance. The path continued past the shelves to an alcove with torches mounted on the wall, illuminating a desk. The desk's occupant furiously scribbled on parchment with a pen.

When the memory of Lucifer attempted to greet him,

the man perked up, then darted from his chair. With a flash of blue light, the creature flew off into the darkness.

"Stop!" the young Lucifer had cried. *"I'm not here to hurt you. I just...I don't even know **why** I'm here."*

"Who is that? Where are we?" asked Raum.

Lucifer gave no response. He hadn't been a willing participant in these revelations up until now and he wasn't about to start. But he remembered well that this was the moment when he had first come into contact with Metatron, the Scribe of Heaven.

Raum watched the scene of Lucifer and Metatron's first meeting play out with interest, but he was also growing impatient.

"Will they get on with it already?" He gestured with his hand and the memory seemed to jump ahead. And then he heard Metatron say something very interesting.

"The seraphim worked a spell, converged their power to gift me with the Sight. From that point on, I could see things no other angel could. They believed it would grant me greater power to serve as a more effective chronicler. But there was an unexpected side-effect they never intended."

"What?" asked Lucifer.

The archai's eyes were filled with fear. *"I saw too much. I saw what they didn't want me to see. And when I chronicled my vision, they knew I'd become a threat to everything they'd built."*

Metatron had then spoken of the story that Divine Choir had constructed about the Presence. And finally, the bombshell phrase that had shattered Lucifer's world back then was replayed once more.

"The problem is this story is just that—a story. It's not history, it's mythology," Metatron had said.

Raum waved his hand and the memory looped, playing back for him so he could be certain of what he'd just heard.

Lucifer watched Raum's face as he processed what he'd just heard. The memory melted away, and they were back in the void.

"It was all a lie from the beginning. No greater power in the universe, and certainly no mandate for Heaven to lord over the universe the way they have." Raum's eyes were vacant, but when he turned them on Lucifer, they started to flash with anger. "And. You. *Knew.*"

"Yes, I did," said Lucifer.

"You perpetuated their lie, did their work for them," said Raum, almost in disbelief. "I knew you'd become a failure, but I never knew to what extent. You violated *everything* you claimed to stand for!"

"You think I came to this decision easily?" asked Lucifer. "I tried to tell Anael and Michael. They rejected me. They thought I was lying or that I'd been corrupted. And I realized that angels—whose only purpose was servitude—would crack if they realized that their entire existence was a lie."

"And what, you thought you were so superior to everyone else?" asked Raum.

"Nothing of the sort," said Lucifer. "Some of us have been able to handle the truth—Abraxas, for one. But when Pyriel learned, he went insane. I realized then that I was right to keep the secret throughout these past eons."

"No, you weren't," said Raum. "You haven't any right to keep the truth from us. We both know the real reason."

"You know nothing," said Lucifer.

"Don't I?"

Raum gestured with his hand and a memory appeared

before them again, one of Metatron speaking to Lucifer.

"Why invent such a fantastic story?" Lucifer had asked.

"For one simple reason—control," said Metatron. *"He who controls gods, controls the believers."*

Raum closed his fist and the memory vanished.

"'He who controls gods, controls the believers,'" he repeated. "You perpetuated the secret for the same reason as the Choir—you wanted control over the Infernal Court. If they all still clung to these notions, they would look upon you as their god. Just as we all had come to once being transformed by Hell into our current states."

"Control was never something I wanted," said Lucifer. "All I wanted was to bring people free will. It's why I lit the spark in humanity, it's why I agreed to lead the rebellion in Heaven."

Raum stepped forward and punched Lucifer. The Morningstar attempted to retaliate, but suddenly, he found his arms restrained. The void dissipated, and they returned back to the cavern in Hell.

"You betrayed us, Morningstar. Continued the work of the Choir because it served your interests," said Raum. "Stepping down may have been the best decision you ever made. But it's clear why you chose Cross as your successor. Not because you thought he was fit for the position, but because you knew he'd maintain the same lie you did. After all, he *was* raised by a cult that serves Heaven."

"I thought a man who represented the best of what demons and humanity could aspire to would be a good leader for a new age. To make things better down here," said Lucifer.

"That's what you say. But Cross hasn't done much other than perpetuate the status quo," said Raum. "It's time for real change to come to Hell. And that requires not only new leadership, but new tactics. We can't hide behind armistices and one-sided treaties that rig the game against us. We need to finally rise up."

Lucifer struggled against his shackles, but it was futile. "Raum, listen to me, you don't know what you're talking about. You're becoming gripped by the same madness that took Abraxas and Pyriel. *This* is why I had to keep the secret!"

"Enough!"

Raum shoved his hand against Lucifer's chest, slamming him against the wall and channeling hellfire into his body. Lucifer screamed as the heat burned his soul to its core. It lasted only a moment, but felt like an eternity. When Raum removed his hand, Lucifer's body still smoldered.

"It's time," said Raum. "First, we take Hell. And then, once we've gathered all the demons in Hell together under one voice, we march on Heaven."

Raum generated a sword of hellfire and plunged it into Lucifer's chest. He screamed again and a sadistic smile spread across Raum's face.

"You've become expendable, Morningstar. Now watch a *real* revolution."

CHAPTER 20

Mara sat quietly in the carriage across from Cross and Lilith. At one point, the two had shared a wild passion, but now Mara couldn't help but noticing that even when they were sitting next to each other, there was a distance between them. Even with his recent change to his old appearance, Cross still seemed a different man than he was before he took the throne. Mara hadn't cared for him much back in those days, but she wasn't sure what to make of this new version of him.

The carriage rolled to a stop and they heard voices coming from outside. The driver was speaking to someone. Then there was a rumbling and the carriage resumed its procession. They must have reached the gates of Beelzebub's realm.

"What are we going to say to him?" asked Mara. "'Hi, I think one of your guys is a traitor'?"

Cross shrugged. "You not a fan of the direct route?"

"She's not wrong," said Lilith. "If you don't handle this diplomatically, Beelzebub may view it as an accusation against him. Like you're saying he's not capable of controlling his own people. And he does *not* like you, so it's best to step carefully."

Cross leaned his head back. "Both of you need to just relax. I'm Mr. Diplomacy."

Lilith and Mara exchanged uncomfortable glances. Cross noticed, but didn't say anything.

The carriage rolled to a stop once again and a moment later, the door opened. Mara emerged first, followed by Lilith, and then Cross stepped out last. Many of the demons who populated Beelzebub's realm were gathered on either side of a path leading up to the castle doors, all having come to see the new King of Hell in person.

"My liege." One of Beelzebub's guards, decked out in chitinous armor, stepped forward and knelt before Cross. "I would be honored to escort you to Lord Beelzebub."

Cross gestured for the guard to stand. "Sure, that's fine. Let's just dispense with the pomp, okay?"

The guard rose and bowed, then spun almost perfectly around and started marching down the path towards the castle. The visitors followed behind him.

"Thought you said Beelzebub hated me?" Cross whispered to Lilith.

"He does," she replied. "But he also knows how to play the game."

The castle doors opened when they approached and the guard led them inside. Any staff within stood near the walls at attention as the trio was led deeper into the castle—up the stairs until eventually they arrived at the top floor. In here was a throne room where Beelzebub's insectoid form sat on a chair that—while it would have been perfect for a person of human-like proportions—hardly seemed like it would be comfortable for someone like him.

"Ahh, here he izzz now, the new King of Hell." Beelzebub waved a thin arm for them to approach. The guard bowed and dismissed himself. "Welcome, sire."

"Good to see you, Bee," said Cross.

"Izzz it?" asked Beelzebub. "I've sent many invitations for you to vizzit my realm, and yet you've never answered a single one."

"Sorry," said Cross. "I'm still figuring out how to do this job."

"Then I am honored that your first royal vizzit is to my humble abode. Now, what is it I can do for you?"

"It's about the Morningstar," said Mara.

Beelzebub's head snapped angrily at her and his eyes burned bright yellow. "Insolent cow! Do not speak before the King of Hell has had his say!"

Mara narrowed her eyes and her hands tightened into fists. She didn't care much for Beelzebub in general, but to have him condescend to her was almost too much to bear. Lilith could clearly sense her feelings as well, because she placed a hand on her shoulder to calm her. Though it went against her every instinct, Mara allowed herself to relax.

"She's just concerned, no offense meant," said Cross. "Thing is, Lucifer has gone missing. Seems the convoy you provided was attacked by raiders. And we'd like to know how Lucifer's presence was even uncovered, let alone his route."

Beelzebub paused before responding and just focused his gaze on Cross. Luther, for his part, remained stoic, his sunglasses concealing his own eyes. After a sufficient amount of sizing each other up, Beelzebub finally spoke.

"Are you saying there'zzz a traitor in my midst?" he asked.

"Beelzebub, we simply want to know what happened to the Morningstar," said Lilith. "We've all heard the rumors of someone gaining followers in the Badlands. And if some of those within the existing realms have been converted, no one would fault you for that."

"You're telling me that I cannot control my own people," said Beelzebub. "That is a fairly significant charge, Lilith."

"It happens to all of us," said Lilith. "No one saw Abraxas's betrayal coming, and he was a Hell Lord in the highest regard."

Beelzebub looked back and forth between the trio. "So what would you have me do, exactly?"

"We'd need to question your people," said Mara. "Anyone who knew that Lucifer and I were here, anyone who knew of our route. These were your men who were killed by the raiders, Beelzebub. Don't you think your denizens might be a bit upset to learn that their lord wouldn't lift a finger to find who betrayed them?"

"That sounds like a threat, little demoness." Beelzebub's gaze drifted back to Cross. "Izzz this how you conduct your business, King? You wish to threaten one of The Fallen with a public smear campaign?"

Cross held up his hands. "Hey now, nobody's threatening anything. What Mara is saying is that you do a lot of work for your subjects."

"Oh yes, indeed I do," said Beelzebub.

"And any good ruler knows that he has to protect his subjects. Should they be killed, a good ruler would see to it that the murderers are brought to justice," said Cross. "So I guess the real question is what kind of ruler *are* you, Beelzebub?"

"Or perhaps there'zzz another explanation," said

Beelzebub. "The Morningstar may have staged his disappearance."

"What are you saying?" asked Mara. "Why would he do that?"

"He *has* been somewhat unstable," said Beelzebub. "And it isn't azzz if he has always had our best interests at heart. After all, he has had a tendency to sell out his own kind on more than one occasion. Lilith would know something about that, would she not?"

Lilith stiffened, but managed to keep her discomfort hidden. "I've made peace with the role Lucifer had in my confinement. He's done damage, there is no denying that. But if we're going to begin to repair that damage, we first need to find him."

"And who can we trust thozzze repairs to?" Beelzebub pointed an appendage at Cross. "The son of a traitor who wazzz appointed as Lucifer's successor?"

"You're starting to hurt my feelings there, Bee," said Cross. "Keep this up, I just might forget to invite you to my birthday party."

"Your taunts matter little to me, half-breed," said Beelzebub.

The color drained from Mara's face as a revelation hit her. Beelzebub's tone had grown increasingly combative. The demon had become like a cornered animal, willing to bite any who came near. And that was telling.

"It wasn't one of your people," said Mara. "It was you."

"What nonsense is this?" asked Beelzebub, and then turned his ire on Lilith. "Control your subject, woman!"

Lilith cast a questioning glance at Mara's direction. With her expressions, she was asking whether her former guard was positive of this. Mara gave a nod to indicate her certainty. And for Lilith, Mara's confidence was enough.

"Mara is one of the finest demons in all of Hell. Her honor is above reproach. It's why I sent her to represent my interests on Earth," said Lilith. "If she believes this, then so do I."

"And you, half-breed king?" asked Beelzebub. "Where do you stand on these accuzzzations?"

"I'd prefer some solid evidence, but I'd say the fact that you keep trying to insult me right to my face isn't really convincing me you're on the level," said Cross.

"Then I'd say our business izzz concluded."

Beelzebub's gossamer wings hefted his form off the throne and he held his arms out to the side. His appendages lit up with hellfire, which quickly left his body and surrounded the trio in a circle of flames that almost reached the ceiling.

"I was one of the first to join Lucifer's rebellion," said Beelzebub. "I did my part to keep him honest, to keep him true to his mission. But he wazzz more interested in maintaining the status quo, in placating the angelzzz he still clearly wanted to be with."

"If you think any of that's true, then you know nothing about the Morningstar," said Mara.

"Don't patronizzze me, child," said Beelzebub. "Lucifer spent eonzzz in Hell, hiding in his tower and resisting the influence of this glorious place. But I, on the other hand, embraced the power of Hell like no other. If there wazzz to be a new King of Hell, it should have been me."

"So what, you're the guy behind what's happening in the Badlands? Trying to stage a revolution?" asked Cross.

"Hardly, I'm simply taking advantage of the situation," said Beelzebub. "Raum is just a meanzzz to an end."

"Raum, of course…" muttered Lilith before casting a glare in Mara's direction. She still had sore memories from when Raum had attempted to overthrow her rule. And with Lucifer's recklessness cracking open Cocytus, now he was back to cause more problems.

"You're dumber than you look, Bee," said Cross. "You think Raum's interested in sharing power with you?"

"Hardly, but he will prove a useful pawn for now," said Beelzebub. "And then, once the time is right, I'll eliminate him and claim *my* destiny as the true King of Hell!"

"Yeah, fuck all that." Cross plunged his hands into the flames. His red eyes began crackling with power behind his sunglasses. The flames started flowing from the circle and into his arms, becoming absorbed by his body. Soon, the hellfire circle was gone, but now Cross had become engulfed by the hellfire. It was so much that he had trouble containing it within his body.

The power was a lot for the cambion to take in. It forced him to his knees and Beelzebub watched with joy on his face.

"You can't do it!" cackled the Hell Lord. "You're too weak, half-breed! Not even the blood of Abraxas could overcome the frailty of that whore human who birthed you!"

Cross's anger reached its peak at that comment. The flames started to subside and though his movements were slow and faced a great deal of resistance, he managed to push himself up on one knee. Then he started to stand.

"No…impossible…" muttered Beelzebub, his eyes widening with fear. "You're nothing more than a half-breed, you shouldn't be capable of resisting the power of The Fallen!"

"Bitch, I went toe-to-toe with the Angel of Death and walked away," said Cross. "So clearly you have no idea who you are fucking with."

Cross channeled Beelzebub's hellfire into his palms and redirected it at the Hell Lord. Beelzebub was quickly immolated by his own power and screamed in terror at the pain as the flames seared his black soul.

"Stop!" said Mara, grabbing Cross's arm. He looked at her and she was startled to see the demon in him coming forth. Horns had already begun to emerge from his head, and when she tried to get in his way, he looked ready to destroy her as well.

"You want some, too?" he asked in a dark, sinister tone.

"If you kill Beelzebub, then we won't know what Raum has done with Lucifer," said Mara. "Like it or not, we need that little shit alive for just a bit longer."

Cross huffed, shook his head, and then channeled the rest of Beelzebub's power up into the ceiling. Once the smoke cleared, his breathing was heavy, but the demon had regressed.

Beelzebub lay on the ground in front of his throne, his insectoid body smoldering. The yellow glow of his eyes was dim, his wings had been burnt off, and his appendages weakly shuddered, the only real sign that he was still alive.

Mara generated a hellfire whip and wrapped it around his throat, then pulled him over to her. In her free hand, she forged a hellfire knife and knelt down beside the demon.

"Now it's my turn," she said.

CHAPTER 21

Raum exited the caverns that he and his followers had been using as their base of operations. Since he'd been able to escape from Cocytus, he'd been building up an army. Some were like him, fellow inmates who had been able to escape the prison's confines. Others had simply been exiled from whatever realm they were initially placed in. And as his movement began to spread, so too did his words breach the walls of the different realms. Offering people another option than the oligarchy that had dominated Hell since the beginning.

And his numbers had swelled to the point that now, he had an army of demons assembled at the mouth of the cave, waiting for his words. His wings emerged from his back and spread out. They raised him above the demons so he could address them all.

"For eons, we've been fed a lie. A lie that told of a false rebellion," said Raum. "The Morningstar was held out above us as a shining revolutionary who had liberated us and given us a land of our own, where we could thrive. Whether you were born angel or human, Hell was initially promised as a realm free of the oppression found both on Earth and in Heaven.

"But that's not what we got. Instead of freedom, we were given chains and torture. The Fallen were so twisted in their hatred for Heaven and so impotent that they had no choice but to take it out on all of us. Even the most benevolent of Hell Lords had become a sadistic bastard."

There were jeers and curses flung from the crowd in agreement with Raum's statements. The demons vocalized their hatred for their overlords and Raum was pleased with the response.

"And where, in all of this, was the great Light-Bringer, who was supposed to help us transcend the limitations of existence? Where was the Morningstar, who we'd always been told was the liberator of all liberators, who had the courage to stand up to the tyrants of Heaven and tell them, 'no'? I'll tell you where he was—hiding in his tower!"

Cheers of agreement swelled up from the demons. Raum paused and allowed them their moment of catharsis. When he was ready to continue, he held up his hands and the crowd's raucous words shrank to a murmur.

"Lucifer spent all that time living in his own private realm. He stood atop his ivory tower—it's *literally* an ivory tower, can you believe that?—and watched. He watched as the Hell Lords who had been his lieutenants during The Fall became twisted, vile creatures that turned their impotent rage on their own people."

Of course, Raum wouldn't mention that he had struck a deal with Beelzebub for support. He had even promised the most twisted demon in Hell a place by his side as an advisor. And Beelzebub was content to be able to indulge his own appetites than be burdened with the responsibility of governance—or so Raum believed.

"Lucifer even went so far as to fraternize with the very

oppressors he'd claimed to despise. He had regular meetings with Gabriel of Heaven. He struck deals with the Divine Choir to preserve an armistice, one which required him to turn on demons like Lilith.

"What was her crime? To be a human who slept with a demon and gave birth to the first cambions. But the angels themselves had engaged in so much fucking and raping that they'd produced the nephilim. And were any of them punished?"

"NO!" the crowd responded in unison.

"Of course they weren't. But Lilith was considered the dangerous one. And so when she came to Hell, she was imprisoned at the behest of the Divine Choir." Raum shook his head. "Even after he rebelled against their tyrannical rule, Lucifer was still bending to their demands.

"And of course, there came Abraxas. One of his own lieutenants. But Lucifer once again turned to Heaven and worked with them to banish the first of The Fallen to join his cause.

"But it gets worse. Because after all this time of being an absentee king, in the face of an angel attempting to create another war, Lucifer then chose to abandon Hell and live among the humans."

More insults and objections were shouted by the gathered demons.

"Now he's back. But did he return because he wanted to make amends? To seek penance for his neglect?" asked Raum. "No, he returned because he lost his powers and wanted them back."

Loud, raucous booing rose up.

"And all this time, do you know what Lucifer has been doing? He's been preserving the greatest lie in the history of creation, a lie concocted by the first seraphim. His discovery of the lie is what led him to rebel. But he chose to keep this knowledge only to himself.

"Would you like to know what this lie is?"

Shouts in the affirmative followed, the gathered demons practically begging Raum to reveal the truth. He waited until their calls died down and then he spoke.

"The Presence is the lie," he said, very simply. "He was never real. There is no great, cosmic power behind the universe. The universe is simply random and chaotic. But the seraphim felt that not even their own brethren could handle this truth. It was, simply put, a method of control."

The crowd became silent, the weight of the realization slowly dawning on them.

"And when Lucifer learned it, he chose to maintain that secret because he feared what would happen if people knew. In fact, he told me as much himself."

Now the crowd responded with anger.

"So why are we preserving these outdated, archaic structures of authority?" asked Raum. "The Fallen are no better than us because they were once angels. The rebellion was just Lucifer's way of taking control for himself. He wanted the same power as the Divine Choir, and so he turned on them to grab that power for himself!

"Well, no more. Because now, we are going to march into the center of Hell. We're going to go right up to that fucking tower of his, and we're going to tear it down!"

The crowd erupted with cheers.

"Spread the word! To those you know in the realms! Let them know the truth of Lucifer's lie! Let them know the hypocrisy of the Infernal Court! Let's rip apart this charade and replace it with something new!"

The demons continued to shout and Raum gestured forth. They began their march towards the center of Hell, where they would do exactly as he said. And Raum waited until the last of them had left. Then he returned to the caverns to visit his prized prisoner.

Lucifer hung on the chains, anger written on his face. "You're a fine one to talk. You rile them up, then let them go off and fight the battle you're too afraid to fight yourself."

"On the contrary," said Raum. "I'm a man of the people, Lucifer. And I'm going to join them in battle. But before I do, I wanted to leave you with a little parting gift."

Raum held out his hands and small spheres of light appeared, flittering out from his palms and growing in size. In the light, Lucifer could see scenes of demons gathering in different realms.

"Did you like my speech? I hope so, because now it's being received by my followers throughout all of Hell. And they're going to show it to others," said Raum. "There's a whiff of rebellion in the air, Morningstar. And you have the privilege of watching it on these orbs. You get to sit there as everything you fought for comes crashing down."

"And then what? What will you do once the tower is gone and the Hell Lords have been removed? Hold free and fair elections? Allow yourself to be stripped of power?" Lucifer scoffed and shook his head. "Somehow, you don't really strike me as the type who's willing to submit to a peaceful transfer of power."

"I'll do what's necessary for the people," said Raum.

"Right, and who decides what's necessary?"

Raum didn't answer. Lucifer gave a nod.

"That's what I thought. You may think me a hypocrite, and in some sense, you could be right," said Lucifer. "But what does that make you?"

"I hope you like your accommodations, because you're never going to leave," said Raum. "You get to watch as my armies tear down your world and build up my own. You'll see The Fallen executed for crimes against their people. But I'm not going to kill you, Lucifer. I want you to remain here in this cave—alone, powerless, chained. Forced to do nothing but watch as I take everything that was once yours.

"Because *that's* exactly what you did to me when you tossed me into your little prison as if I were just some insignificant piece of garbage."

Lucifer scoffed. "That's because you *were* just some insignificant piece of garbage. Still are, in fact."

Raum's eyes narrowed in anger. He backhanded Lucifer. The Morningstar's head was rocked by the blow and it left a mark along the side of his face. He stretched out his jaw a few times to try and work it through the pain.

"Enjoy the show, *angel*," said Raum, hissing that last word. "It promises to be a good one."

Raum left Lucifer alone in his cave. The pain Lucifer felt from the blow was nothing in comparison to what he was watching unfold on the little screens Raum had conjured.

The armies marched across the Badlands, gathering more as they moved closer to the center. Riots had broken out across the different realms, and the forces commanded by the Hell Lords were struggling to regain some sense of order. But even amongst their own security forces, Lucifer watched as open rebellion gripped the land.

Lucifer was witnessing the end of the Hell that he had built. But he had brought this all upon himself. He thought back to that fateful day when he encountered Metatron for the first time. That tiny little angel had warned him, even back then.

"I know you want your freedom, but this path will only make you even more of a servant to the Choir."

Did he know, even back then, what would happen if Lucifer rebelled? The final words Metatron spoke before Lucifer dismissed him and went off on his arrogant quest now rang loud in the Morningstar's memory.

"For every action, there is a reaction. What you are thinking of doing has never been done before—never even been contemplated before. There is no way to know for certain what the result will be."

Maybe he didn't know precisely what would have happened. Maybe there was no way for Lucifer to be warned about this. But Metatron knew that *something* would happen. After The Fall, Lucifer had reflected on the Scribe's warning. At the time, he simply assumed Metatron had been talking about his exile into Hell.

But in retrospect and after everything that had happened since, it seemed Metatron was actually talking about this moment right here and now. Raum was right about one thing—Lucifer *was* a hypocrite. He spoke of the importance of knowledge, then kept the greatest secret in existence. His own anger at the Choir's arrogance had been twisted and he adopted their same rationale. His talk of free will was undermined by allowing the Hell Lords to rule as the despots they were. And for all his talk of responsibility, he'd still been trying to avoid it. By ignoring his duties as king, by running off to Earth and allowing Cocytus to crack open—all of it on him.

As he watched the chaos unfold, he thought of Anael. How different might things have been if he hadn't let his arrogance get the better of him? If he had simply found a different way?

His world was falling apart and he had brought it all on himself.

CHAPTER 22

We don't know how much time we've got before Beelzebub's guards start getting suspicious," said Mara. "If I'm going to properly interrogate him, I need a place where I can't be disturbed."

"Understood." In hushed tones, Lilith began whispering in the language of the damned. Her fingers flexed and retracted in specific ways as her hands made deliberate motions, drawing invisible lines in the air. Trails of energy started to follow her movements, and then she worked her arms into it, creating big, sweeping motions with them. The energy trails crossed together, forming a large mass that quickly grew into a portal back to her domain.

"Go, now," said Lilith. "I have to be the last one through or else the portal will close with me."

Cross picked up Beelzebub's unconscious form and went through first, then Mara jumped into the portal right after him. Lilith could hear voices coming from outside the throne room. Beelzebub's guards were on the move. She jumped into the portal last and it closed behind her just as they came through the doors.

The portal had led directly to Lilith's own palace. They were greeted by Kragmor, who was sitting on Lilith's throne and talking to himself. He looked surprised by their sudden appearance.

"M-mistress!" he yelped. "I wasn't expecting you back so soon! And with guests, no less!"

Kragmor hopped off the throne and flittered over in front of Cross. He landed and then bowed in supplication.

"O great King Cross, it is an honor to be in your presence!" said Kragmor.

Cross slid his sunglasses down his nose and then cast a look of annoyance in Lilith's direction.

"Yes, he's always like this," said Lilith. "Get up, Kragmor."

Kragmor stood and brushed himself off. "I'm surprised to see you here so soon. What with all the trouble."

"What trouble?" asked Mara.

Kragmor then told them about the uprisings that had started to occur in domains all around Hell and more than that, about the speech that Raum had managed to broadcast to his followers. A speech that was being shared with other demons as well.

"Are we experiencing uprisings, too?" asked Lilith.

Kragmor nodded. "It's not as dire as other areas, but yes, we have had some riots break out."

"Shit…" muttered Cross. "This is exactly what Lucifer was afraid would happen."

"So it's true?" asked Kragmor. "The Morningstar really helped maintain the secrets of the Divine Choir?"

"It's true, and I suppose that's something we'll have to deal with," said Cross. "Meantime, we've got to get this under control. Lil, any chance you can zap me back to my tower? I gotta be there to coordinate a response and be ready once Raum turns up."

"Yes, of course," said Lilith. "But there's still the matter of Lucifer's whereabouts."

"Give me a room alone with him and I'll know everything he does in no time," said Mara.

"You sure about that?" asked Cross. "He *is* one mean sonnuva bitch."

"Maybe so, but he started off as an angel and then became a Hell Lord. He's never actually experienced torture firsthand," said Mara.

"Once you find his location, I'll have to send you on your own," said Lilith.

"Of course, you've got your own realm to worry about," said Mara. "The Morningstar brought me along to protect him, so I have to fulfill my obligation."

Cross passed Beelzebub's unconscious body to Mara. Lilith opened a portal for him back to the tower. No words were exchanged, he simply walked through the portal and it closed after him.

"Find out what Beelzebub knows quickly," Lilith told Mara. "If you need any help—"

"I'm fine," said Mara. "You'll need all the help you can get."

Beelzebub had actually confessed to Raum's location in a very short amount of time. True to her word, Lilith provided a portal as close as she could get to the caverns in the Badlands where Raum had been gathering his forces. And she also provided Mara with some armor that would provide protection against any forces that remained behind.

Mara emerged from the portal and could see the caverns not far off in the distance. There was no other activity, though. Raum was making good on his threat to storm the center of Hell with his legions, and seemed he didn't leave many behind.

As Mara approached, she could sense Lucifer's presence nearby. Without his powers, the signal was definitely weak, but it was still unmistakably him. She broke into a run for the caves.

When she came closer, she saw there were a few guards who remained. Mara's wings erupted from her back and she launched from the ground. She hovered above the caverns, trying to get a sense of the layout. Two guards were stationed at the ground-level entrance and didn't seem like there was any other way inside.

Mara flew back down, landing on one of the jutting structures from the side of the mountain. Only two raiders, she could handle them without any trouble. She jumped from her perch and used her wings to increase the speed of her descent. She crashed down into one of the guards, flattening him on the surface.

"Hey!" The other guard held a massive war-hammer and swung it.

Mara jumped over the swing, spun, and kicked him in the head. The attack barely stunned him, and when she landed, he was already bringing the hammer down on top of her head. She threw her arms up, a hellfire shield forming just in time to block the attack.

The guard pulled his hammer away and stepped back. He stomped on the ground in frustration. Mara lowered the shield and gave a smirk as she beckoned the guard with a finger.

"What kind of people does Raum have working for

him anyway?" she asked. "Two of you can't handle one little demon?"

"Bitch, I'll *show* you what I can handle!"

The guard charged her. Mara stood waiting, as if she wasn't aware of the stampeding demon barreling down on her. She jumped away at the very last second, throwing out a thin hellfire cable.

The guard ran right into the cable and it caught his neck. Mara quickly looped it around a few more times and pulled tightly on both ends. The guard collapsed to his knees, struggling against the cable, while Mara just kept pulling it tighter and tighter.

And then, the cable became slack. The guard's body collapsed on the ground. His head rolled to a stop right near Mara. She gave it a kick and then went into the cavern.

"Lucifer?" she called. "Lucifer!"

No response came. Mara closed her eyes and focused on Lucifer's presence. She was able to pick up the signal and went towards it. The cavern was a maze of tunnels and passages, and she encountered more than a few dead-ends in her search. But she was at least making progress, and she could feel his presence growing stronger.

Eventually she did come to a spot where his presence felt the strongest. Mara channeled her hellfire into her fist and delivered a blow to shatter the stone door. Inside was a small alcove and Lucifer hung from the wall, his arms and legs restrained by shackles. All around him were small spheres of light, transmitting images.

"Lucifer!" Mara called as she entered. She ran over to him, but then looked at the spheres. They were scenes of demons battling each other and large-scale riots. Structures being destroyed, beasts running free.

"It's the fall of Hell," said Lucifer. "And it's all my fault."

"Let's get you out of here." Mara went over to Lucifer's side and broke open the shackles around his legs first so he could stand under his own power and then she released his arms. "Now come on, we have to get to Cocytus before—"

She had started to return to the entrance, but stopped when she realized Lucifer hadn't moved.

"Lucifer?"

Lucifer rubbed his wrists from the strain of being shackled. "I'm not going to Cocytus."

"But your powers…"

"What good would it do if I got them back? If I even *could* get them back?" he asked.

"You could stop Raum from tearing down Hell."

"Why?" asked Lucifer. "Hell was built on a lie, no different from Heaven. Raum was right about that. And now, I'm paying for the consequences of my actions."

Mara walked over to him. "This isn't paying for anything. This is you hiding in a cave, feeling sorry for yourself. You're not dealing with the consequences, you're running away from them."

"It doesn't matter anymore," said Lucifer. "It's all over now. Raum will destroy the Court and he'll set up his own rule. Why should I even care? I never acted as a king should. I let Heaven write the rules and control the narrative while I did everything I possibly could to avoid facing any responsibility."

"And how is this any different?" asked Mara. "You're still evading. Still hiding away. You traded a tower in the center of Hell for a mansion on Earth and then traded that for a cave in the Badlands. If you want to face up to the consequences of your actions, then you can do that. But do it on *your* terms. Face up to the people yourself. Letting a despot like Raum burn down Hell isn't any sort of penance. It's just more evasion."

Lucifer looked at the different spheres hovering around him. These were his people, this was his home. If he let Raum take it all away, his entire existence would become an absolute waste. He had to stand up and take action while he still could.

"Go to Cocytus, get my powers back, and then what?" asked Lucifer.

"Isn't that up to you…" asked Mara, "…sire?"

Determination overcame Lucifer's features. His hands curled into fists and he held his head up.

"Then I have to go about setting things right. And I believe I know exactly how to do that," said Lucifer. "But first, I need to get my powers back. I hope you have a way to get us to Cocytus."

Mara nodded and reached beneath her armor. She drew out a small coin. "Cross gave me this, it will open a portal directly to Cocytus. And then you can find out what you have to do next."

Lucifer took the coin from Mara and examined it. It was marked with a sigil that represented Cocytus itself. He could feel the energy inside the coin. He only hoped that this truly would lead him to Erebus and a way out of this mess.

The Morningstar threw the coin and it expanded in mid-air, the metal dissolving away and leaving an open portal in its place with a ring of ethereal energy around the edges.

"Do you want me to come with you?" she asked.

Lucifer shook his head. "No. I think it would be better

if I do this on my own. I doubt Erebus will be happy if I bring any uninvited guests along for the ride."

He stepped to the edge of the portal and looked inside. Already he could feel the cold emanating from the remains of Cocytus. He had no idea what would greet him on the other end, or if Erebus would even be willing to speak to him. But no one ever said that facing consequences would be easy.

Lucifer stepped into the portal and was instantly transported to the location of Cocytus.

CHAPTER 23

Cocytus was located in the deepest pit of Hell. The prison was a frozen lake that extended down to the reaches of infinity. Once trapped within the waters of Cocytus, a prisoner would be frozen in a state of suspended animation. Unable to move or react with the outside world in any way. But they would remain conscious the entire time—confined for eternity.

The prison was watched by the demon called Erebus. His body consisted of an exoskeleton of twisted and pointed bones, his head the shape of a goat's skull with giant horns protruding from the sides. He stood at the banks that met the frozen water and knelt before them, one hand clutching his staff.

"Morningstar," he said in a deep voice without turning. He could sense the presence of his former master. "I had wondered if you would ever return to this place."

"Unfortunately, circumstances had kept me away," said Lucifer. "Hello, Erebus. It's been a long time."

"Eons, in fact." Erebus pushed his weight on his staff as he stood to face Lucifer. When he looked at the fallen angel, Erebus's eyes briefly flashed yellow and he tilted his head at an angle. "But you are different than you were back then. Lesser in some ways."

Lucifer frowned. "Yes. I'm afraid an encounter with one of the escapees left me powerless."

"Perhaps a suitable consequence given your role in those escapes."

Lucifer took a step closer. "I know I have much to answer for. Had I known at the time that abdicating the throne would weaken Cocytus, I would have—"

"Would have what?" asked Erebus by way of interruption. "Would have put off your desire to escape? Would have remained in Hell to live up to your responsibilities?"

Lucifer sighed. "If we're being completely honest here, then I truly don't know. But I doubt it."

Erebus gave a slow nod. "As I thought. Though I do appreciate the candor."

"But I'm here now," said Lucifer. "And Raum has brought chaos to Hell. If I had my powers back, I believe I could stop him."

"You do? When not even the combined might of the Infernal Court seems capable? What makes you so special?"

"Hell's power comes from me. If I'm one with it again, then I can turn the tide. Provide the people a reason to stop this insane revolution."

"If you could, what will happen to Cocytus? To Raum? To Hell itself?"

"Before I tell you that, just answer me one question—is it possible for my powers to be restored?" asked Lucifer.

Erebus looked out over the frozen lake, which was littered with cracks and outright breaks, revealing still, icy waters beneath.

"Cocytus was born from you. It is the last remaining

vestige of your power. So yes, I believe it could," said Erebus. "Now it's your turn to answer my questions."

"My answer is I don't know," said Lucifer. "But that's because I don't think those decisions should be up to me anymore. I've failed in my role as the King of Hell. I have no right to the throne anymore, no claim to the title. And if demons like Raum are to be held accountable, then so should I."

Erebus gave a chuckle that sounded like nails scraping against metal. It was obvious that he didn't believe Lucifer's words. But as he laughed, he looked at the Morningstar, saw the grim expression on his face, and he realized just how serious Lucifer truly was.

"You mean it, don't you?" asked the demon. "You truly are willing to surrender yourself to the mercy of Hell's denizens and accept whatever judgment they put upon your head."

Lucifer nodded. "It's time I accepted responsibility for my actions. I've lived under the threat of the Divine Choir's retaliation for far too long. I never had any business ruling Hell. It wasn't a job I wanted and certainly not one I took seriously."

"Very well, then I shall help you." Erebus raised his staff and pointed it at the frozen lake. "If you are to be restored, then you and Cocytus must be one again. To absorb its power, you must destroy the prison."

"But aren't there still prisoners inside? Ones who haven't escaped?" asked Lucifer.

Erebus nodded. "That is the price. To be restored, you have to release those you imprisoned."

"Raum, Barbatos, Astaroth. You've seen what they did

when they were released. How will letting them all go free make things better?"

"Maybe it won't. But you will have to face those consequences, too. You can't repair the damage by continuing to pick at the wounds."

Lucifer looked out at the frozen lake. Destroying Cocytus was one step closer to eliminating his legacy. It'd be a difficult path to walk, but change could only come if he was willing to let go of those old structures. He moved to the edge of the bank and took a careful step forward onto the ice.

It was slippery and he had to hold his arms out to balance himself as he carefully took another step. And then another and another. Before long, Lucifer was standing in the middle of the ice, facing one of the giant holes and the frigid water beneath. He gave one last look at Erebus, who nodded.

Lucifer looked back at the water and jumped, diving beneath its surface. The intensity of the cold was unlike anything he'd ever felt before. This was beyond freezing and a completely different feeling from having his soul seared by hellfire or even soulfire.

Down amongst the depths, Lucifer opened his eyes and looked around. He could see them all, the prisoners that remained in Cocytus. Each one frozen in a perpetual state of solitary confinement. None of them able to do anything but reflect on what they'd done in their lives and how they could look forward to nothing in the future. Just an eternity of stagnation.

In some ways, it was the same fate Lucifer faced before he made the choice to abdicate the throne. And if he wanted to change his fate, they should be entitled to the same.

He created this place due to political pressure, because he didn't want to risk further angering the Divine Choir. So fearful was he of another war that he surrendered Hell's sovereignty. And these beings, they were the ones who paid the price.

Perhaps some of them *did* deserve a place in Cocytus. But it wasn't the Morningstar's role to unilaterally make that decision. There would have to be some sort of justice done. Not on the basis of politics or fear, but out of impartiality.

Lucifer held his arms out to the sides and he concentrated, shutting his eyes. He allowed himself to feel every spot on his body where the frigid water touched. It seeped into his pores, burrowing beneath his skin. And as he remained immersed in Cocytus, he could feel its power beginning to merge with his own soul.

A spark was lit deep within him. Lucifer opened his eyes, the pale yellow color now replaced by a healthy, golden glow. The prison's energy continued to move into his body, and the glow intensified. Cracks began to appear in the remaining ice and the prisoners held stationary within were able to begin to move. The ice continued to break along those faults and started shattering.

A halo of light emerged from within Lucifer's body. The inverted pentagram that Abraxas has once painted on his chest before The Fall appeared again, as if it were made of fire. The remaining ice broke apart and melted, becoming one with the water. And the water itself?

It started boiling.

The banks over Cocytus were filled with the steam of the evaporating lake. Erebus watched as the water faded away, leaving barren land and the prone forms of the remaining prisoners beginning to stir for the first time since they were frozen.

Lucifer himself remained at the center, hovering above the ground. Wings forged of flame emerged from his back and took shape. The last of Cocytus's energy was absorbed into him and he landed on the ground where Erebus moved forward to meet him.

"It seems to have worked," said the now-former warden.

Lucifer folded his wings forward, marveling at their return. He had thought he'd never see them again, forgotten what it felt like to possess them even. The power of Cocytus coursed through his soul, fueling him and giving him strength. And now, the time had come to complete his mission and begin the next phase of his journey.

The Morningstar launched from the ground and his wings pushed him up through the levels of Hell, headed towards the center where his enemy waited.

CHAPTER 24

Raum's army had made it to the center of Hell and the tower where the current king, Luther Cross, kept his residence. Just as Lucifer before him, Cross had made the decision to be a leader separated from everything. Any attempts to institute some kinds of reforms were met with resistance from the Infernal Court. But Raum didn't know nor care about any of that. He was more interested in achieving his own goals.

Cross did command some guard forces that monitored the barrier to his domain, but they were quickly overwhelmed by the sheer numbers of Raum's raiders. They tore through the security in short order and by the time Cross had returned to try to intercept Raum himself, they had already breached the tower.

It was a valiant attempt, but by the time it had gotten this far, it was too little, too late. Raum's time in the Badlands since escaping from Cocytus had obviously not only been spent on giving speeches, but also improving his own skills. And Cross hadn't been in a fight since before he accepted the throne, which had dulled his combat instincts and fighting prowess. Not even the power he commanded as the king were enough to deal with Raum.

Cross lay on the ground, his body utterly battered by Raum. The demon held a long, flaming lance in his hand, looked down at the current king, and just shook his head in disappointment.

"Maybe it's a good thing that your father isn't here to see this," said Raum. "I can't imagine Abraxas would be happy at seeing how his own son had utterly failed so spectacularly."

Cross's red eyes flashed and he spoke a single word: "*Ignis!*"

A small explosion formed right in front of Raum and he was thrown through the tower's window. His wings flared to life and caught the air, holding him in place. Raum kept himself aloft and waited for Cross to step up to the window. But the cambion remained there, not choosing to pursue him further. And Raum laughed.

"Look at you, so terrified to embrace your nature," he said. "You could easily conjure up your own wings and come after me. But you're still too tied to your own humanity, aren't you? That's why you won't win."

A great burst of bright, golden light appeared above the tower. It blinded both Raum and Cross and briefly brought a cessation to the battle by their forces on the ground. Raum held his hand over his eyes to try and provide some protection to them.

The light was so powerful, it could be seen all throughout Hell. And as it faded, the most beautiful angel in creation was left hovering above the tower, wearing a black suit and his vibrant, yellow eyes framed by halos of bright, golden energy.

"I think we've all had quite enough of your antics, Raum," said the Morningstar.

"Lucifer?" asked Raum. "This isn't possible. I left you chained up in a cave, powerless!"

"Perhaps next time you should try killing your opponent instead of keeping them around to gloat," said Lucifer.

"Oh believe me, that's a mistake I'll surely rectify!"

Raum's wings launched him at Lucifer and he held his lance in both hands, pointing the blade in front of him. Lucifer remained hovering above and flames coursed from his chest and into his palms. Two long swords forged of hellfire in his grasp. When Raum reached him, Lucifer blocked his lance by crossing the blades in front of his body.

"How did you escape? How are your powers back?" Raum demanded.

"If I were you, I'd be less concerned about how we got to this point and instead focus on the battle," said Lucifer.

Undeterred from the first block, Raum reforged his weapon into a large broadsword that he swung at Lucifer. The Morningstar crossed his blades against the broadsword and held it in place.

"You're pretty good, Raum, I have to give you that," said Lucifer. "But despite your strength, I was still trained by the likes of Michael and Azrael."

Lucifer channeled his power into the swords and worked them together. Raum was surprised to see his long, wide blade beginning to buckle under the pressure. Lucifer broke Raum's sword in two.

The Morningstar flew back and hurled his swords. They cut through the air and each stabbed one of Raum's wings. The demon cried out and tried to stay in the air, but the wings were too weak.

Lucifer dove after him and grabbed Raum by his collar.

He held him up and stared at him with burning, yellow eyes.

"I'm afraid it won't be that easy."

Lucifer's entire body began to glow and the aura expanded to include Raum as well. Raum felt his soul burning from the inside-out. And then his entire body exploded with flames.

"No!" Raum screamed as he broke away. He pulled the hellfire swords from his wings, but still his flying was erratic. He attempted to pick up speed to put out the fire.

"It's no use, Raum. Your very soul is on fire and it will take a lot more than some bad flying to put it out," said Lucifer.

Raum zig-zagged all over the crimson sky, a bright, yellow streak cutting through the red. He was desperate to prove Lucifer wrong, to quench the fire that was burning his very essence. He screamed the whole time and eventually came to a stop by crashing into the battlefield, right in the midst of the war his own followers were fighting on his behalf.

Lucifer casually lowered from on high, still keeping himself a good distance above the fray. Raum thrashed about, screaming for aid. The spectacle only caused the demons to give him a wide berth as they watched his flailing.

"Put it out! Help!"

Lucifer folded his arms over his chest and smirked. "The great Raum, would-be liberator, but he can't even stand up to a bit of hellfire."

"This is more than hellfire! You did something to me!" screamed Raum.

Lucifer held out a hand and closed it into a fists. The flames vanished, leaving Raum's body blackened and crisp, with smoke still rising from it. He then grabbed Raum by the neck and carried him up into the air, flying to the tower's peak. Lucifer held Raum up to his level so he could see the same thing.

"Have a look at it, Raum. When we first landed here, I saw a desolate landscape that was supposed to be our punishment. No more Elysium fields. No more endless blue sky. Just darkness and despair all around," said Lucifer. "But I thought I could turn that into something better than it was. I believed we could create a counterpoint to Heaven. They had beauty, yet it was only under heavy restriction. I thought to myself, maybe it won't be pretty. But at the very least, it will be free of that restricting order."

"And how did that work out for you?" asked Raum.

"I was an idiot," said Lucifer. "In my arrogance, I thought my knowledge put me above everyone else, including my brethren in The Fallen. Perhaps a part of me *wanted* to keep the secret. There's something to be said about being the keeper of forbidden knowledge—it holds a certain kind of power. I suppose I let that power corrupt me in some small way."

Lucifer glanced at his feathered wings. "You know, for the longest time, I thought I had kept my original wings because the Divine Choir felt it was a unique punishment—a constant reminder of what I'd lost. But you said that I was still doing their bidding. And in a way, you were right.

"Metatron had warned me that if I went down this path, I would become even more of a servant of Heaven. I gave them the pretext they needed to turn me into the villain of the story. God versus the Devil, the ultimate tale of good versus evil. Didn't matter that there was no actual hero in the story or that the villain wasn't exactly evil. That was the narrative they chose and I allowed them to perpetuate it because I felt the most important thing was to avoid another war. Maybe I was wrong to do that."

Lucifer took a deep breath.

"Despite all your transgressions, I do have to thank you for exposing my own hypocrisy," said Lucifer. "I was wrong to imprison you. I had dealt with my problems in the same manner that the Choir dealt with theirs—just lock them away and hope they stay buried."

Lucifer released his grip on Raum but kept him aloft with telekinetic abilities. He used his hands to manipulate Raum's body, so the demon hovered right in front of him.

"However, all that being said, you *do* still pose a danger," said Lucifer. "You may have exposed the flaws in this system I created, Raum. But that doesn't make you the hero of the story. I know what your intentions are for this place. You'd be no different from the Choir or Abraxas or Thanatos. You're just another in a long line of despots twisting justifiable anger and frustration into a tool so you can grab more power. And I can't allow that to happen."

"What are you doing?" asked Raum as he tried to struggle against the invisible hold Lucifer held on his body.

"There's a lot of work to be done," said Lucifer. "When this is all over, there *will* be a new Hell. Unfortunately, it's not a place you'll ever get to see, nor is it a place you would particularly like."

Lucifer held out his hands and placed them on the sides of Raum's head. The demon struggled against the Morningstar's grip, but he was weak from the battle and Lucifer was far stronger. Their respective roles from just a short time earlier had now completely reversed.

"Last time, I made the mistake of thinking you could

simply be locked away. And you made the same mistake with me," said Lucifer. "And it's one that neither of us will make again."

Golden auras appeared around Lucifer's hand. A light shimmered deep within Raum's body. That grew larger, and Lucifer hovered back as the light consumed Raum. He started to scream as he felt the power coursing in every inch of his soul, stretching throughout his body.

"No!" he screamed in protest. "You can't do this to me!"

"It's already done."

Raum's screams continued to rise in tone and urgency. Lucifer just remained hovering there, watching as his light completely engulfed the demon. The would-be usurper to the throne was atomized by the Morningstar's power and not a single semblance of his form was left in its wake.

Lucifer returned to the tower where Cross was leaning against the wall for support, having watched the entire battle play out. As the Morningstar entered the tower that had once been his, Cross just watched him with awe and some mixture of fear.

"That was…pretty spectacular," he said. "Though I've gotta ask what's going to happen now. You said something about a new Hell. What exactly did you mean by that?"

Lucifer cast his gaze around the tower. "This place was built out of my own hubris. Same as Cocytus. I thought I could be a god without actually doing any of the work. And now I realize how wrong-headed I was to think such a thing."

"So what, then?" asked Cross. "You want the throne back? Because honestly, you can have it. I'm anxious to get back to my home."

"Not just yet, Luther. There's still something else I need

you to do before you leave Hell behind completely."

"And what would that be?"

"I built Cocytus to appease the Choir. I let them get away with just about anything they wanted because I was terrified of another war. But worse than all of that is I perpetuated the very lie that sparked my rebellion in the first place," said Lucifer. "Raum was right to expose me. But that's just the first step. I need to make amends and for that to happen, I have to be judged."

"Judged by whom exactly?" asked Cross.

"By Hell." Lucifer looked at Luther Cross with an intensity in his eyes. "I need you to put me on trial for crimes against the denizens of Hell."

EPILOGUE

Since her dismissal by Uriel, Anael hadn't felt the need to return to Heaven. Even she thought her reluctance was strange. She had so resisted being sent to Earth in the first place. But now that Uriel had essentially fired her, she had no reason to remain. Lucifer was back in Hell and she had no purpose on this blue orb.

However, she still found herself staying behind in Chicago. It had been a few weeks since then and she spent her days lounging in The Green Mill. It was a cocktail lounge located in the Uptown neighborhood, and she'd heard Gabriel mention it a few times as one of his favorite locations.

Anael didn't really care one way or the other for the music. But the only other place she knew of was Lust and she was fairly certain that the clientele in that club would object to an angel in their midst.

She sat at a lone table and sipped her gin and tonic, while ignoring the sounds of the live band. A few men did attempt to approach her since she arrived, but she'd blown all of them off. Anael had no interest in interacting with any of them.

"Interesting to find you here."

She sighed and was about to respond negatively. But

when the person speaking to her sat down in the seat across, Anael was surprised to see it was Mara. Her surprise instantly turned to annoyance.

"What are you doing here?" she asked.

"Belial told me what happened," said Mara. "I'm sorry."

"No you're not."

Mara gave a soft chuckle. "No, I suppose I'm not. But seemed like the thing to say."

"I'm not even interested in real sincerity, so you can imagine my feelings on the fake variety," said Anael. "Now can you just leave me in peace?"

"I'll be on my way soon enough. But I came to ask you about something first."

Anael sighed and took another sip of her drink. She set the glass down and flashed her blue eyes across the table. "If I say yes, will you promise to leave me alone? I've pretty much had my fill of both angels *and* demons these days."

"I promise," said Mara. "Just a few minutes of your time and then regardless of your answer, I'll be on my way."

Anael gave a wave of her hand, a gesture for Mara to get on with what she came to say.

"As you know, the Morningstar is back in Hell," said Mara.

"So I'm told. You lot must be over the moon."

"Not exactly," said Mara. "It came at something of a cost. Things are kind of a mess down there right now."

"Maybe you should be talking to Uriel, then. I'm sure he'd be more than happy to give you some ideas on what could be done with the place."

"We have some already and that's why I'm here. There was an uprising."

Anael pretended to be disinterested, but in truth, it

did pique her curiosity. "Hell is a chaotic place. Hardly surprising."

"Lucifer was able to stop it. Got his powers back, took out the instigator, and now—"

"And now everything's back to normal. The Adversary's constant whining about freedom from responsibility was all just a waste of everyone's time," said Anael. "I'll try to hide my surprise."

"Actually, no," said Mara. "Lucifer has surrendered himself."

"Surrender?" Anael couldn't hide her interest any longer. "What do you mean? Surrendered to Heaven?"

Mara shook her head. "To Hell. Or more accurately, to the *people* of Hell."

Anael leaned forward. "What game is he playing now?"

"He blames himself for all of it. The rebellion, Abraxas, Lilith, Cocytus, Astaroth—he's holding himself accountable. He wants to be put on trial for his crimes. To be judged by the people of Hell. And it's very likely there will be people who aren't happy about it—people of the wing-and-halo variety."

Anael shrugged. "Why do you think anyone in Heaven would care? The Adversary is back in Hell where he belongs."

"Because of what he says is his greatest crime—keeping the Divine Choir's secret."

"Secret? What are you babbling about?"

Mara's gaze intensified. "I think you know *exactly* what I'm talking about. You were one of the few he told. But now, Raum has let everyone in Hell in on that secret."

Anael's face went ashen. She of course remembered when Lucifer told her that the Presence did not actually exist, but was simply a creation by the Divine Choir to control the angels. Back then, she balked at such a notion, finding it utterly ridiculous. She hadn't thought about that in ages, still thinking it was some lie Lucifer had told her. Now she was beginning to doubt that.

"Raum broadcast the truth all across Hell. Every demon now knows the truth. And you know it won't be long before word spreads to Heaven as well," said Mara.

Anael shrugged and picked up her drink. "I don't get it. What does any of this have to do with me? If he's telling the truth, then that's a problem for the Choir to deal with. And if he's lying, then it's now become Hell's problem."

"As I said, Lucifer wants to be put on trial. To plead his case before the people of Hell and then accept whatever judgment they impose on him," said Mara. "But every case needs a defense. And Lucifer has said that the only defense he'll accept is yours."

The glass slipped from Anael's grasp and shattered on the lounge floor.

To be continued…

AFTERWORD

When I sat down to plan this book, I had a pretty rough idea of what I wanted to do—Lucifer returning to Hell. That was where we left him off at the end of the last book, after all.

But then I asked myself a question that really helped form the foundation of this story—what if Lucifer didn't want to go back? And that seemed to fit with his character. Lucifer as I've been writing him has been evading responsibility pretty much his entire life. And even though he's realized he needs to take more responsibility for his actions, there's always that push and pull between what you know you should do and what you actually want to do.

So I came up with the idea of Lucifer's lack of responsibility coming back to haunt him. This also gave me the opportunity to pick up on another character introduced in the *Luther Cross* books—and that's Raum. In the larger scheme of things, he was a minor character when he appeared. But he seemed to be the perfect fit for this story.

I'm very happy with the way this book turned out. I feel like this book especially marks a huge turning point in Lucifer's development. And I'm excited to see just where the character will go in the next book.

That book is on its way. The gears in my head are already turning for what will be called *Lucifer Judged*. See you then!

Percival Constantine
March 2021
Kagoshima, Japan

ABOUT THE AUTHOR

Born and raised in the Chicagoland area, Percival Constantine grew up on a fairly consistent diet of superhero comics, action movies, video games, and TV shows. At the age of ten, he first began writing and has never really stopped.

Percival has been working in publishing since 2005 in various capacities—author, editor, formatter, letterer—and has written books, short stories, comics, and more. He has a Bachelor of Arts in English and Mass Media from Northeastern Illinois University and a Master of Arts in English and Screenwriting from Southern New Hampshire University. He currently resides in southern Japan, where he teaches literature and film while continuing to write.

SEE HOW THE FALL BEGAN!

MORNINGSTAR
BOOK 0

LUCIFER
FALLEN

PERCIVAL CONSTANTINE

LUCIFER.PERCIVALCONSTANTINE.COM

**VISIT PERCIVALCONSTANTINE.COM
FOR MORE THRILLING TALES!**

Printed in Great Britain
by Amazon